SAME PLAY, DIFFERENT ACTORS

A William Adams Thriller

Ian Walker

Thomas & Mercer

Copyright © 2024 Ian Walker

All rights reserved.

The right of Ian Walker to be identified as the Author of the Work has been asserted by him in accordance with the Copyright, Designs and Patents Act 1988.

The characters and events portrayed in this book are fictitious. Any similarity to real persons, living or dead, is coincidental and not intended by the author.

No part of this book may be reproduced, or stored in a retrieval system, or transmitted in any form or by any means, electronic, mechanical, photocopying, recording, or otherwise, without express written permission of the publisher.

Published by Thomas & Mercer, Seattle

Amazon, the Amazon logo, and Thomas & Mercer are trademarks of Amazon.com, Inc., or its affiliates.

ISBN-13: 9798329442038

Cover design by: Art Painter
Library of Congress Control Number: 2018675309
Printed in the United States of America

*For Ali and Alex
with love*

CHAPTER 1

Everyone was consoling.

He wanted for nothing: he could have had company around the clock if he'd not refused the many offers of would-be houseguests, or shooed those who escaped his refusals out the door. His fridge was stocked with easy-to-heat casseroles, cooked lovingly on his behalf. The phone rang daily, interrupting his private grief, but often he let it ring out, not up to facing the awkward *bonhomie* contrived at the other end of the line. The mundane tasks and routines of the daily round diverted his grudging attention only long enough to be desultorily attended to.

Although in these various ways his joyless life was filled, he swam in a morass of confused and utter misery.

Nothing was consoling.

He wanted for everything: for the touch of her naked body against his as they lay in bed at night; for the promise of a child to cement their love, in her swelling belly and breasts; for the quiet intercourse of humdrum pleasantries in which they passed the days; for the deep ache of love in just being with her.

◆ ◆ ◆

It was approaching dusk. He sat with his full tumbler of whisky half-drunk, looking thoughtlessly at the Sydney harbour traffic making its way to Circular Quay or Milson's Point or Mosman or Manly or Double Bay.

He answered the phone automatically, without thinking he'd prefer not to speak with anyone.

'William, it's Ross Farnsom.'

Farnsom had been best man at his wedding; the man who stayed with him to search for her when Gill had gone missing; who'd nursed them both following her rape, and later, her death.

'Oh ... Hello, Ross.'

'I'll be there in ten minutes.'

Silence.

'Are you there, William?'

'Yes ... I'm here, Ross ... I'm not really up to anything ... if you don't mind.'

'I do mind and I'll see you soon,' and with that he rang off.

Most days, Ross forced his way into William's flagging consciousness, trying to divert his attention from the depths of loss and to fill his time with a love forged in tribulation and despair.

William was waiting at the door when Ross pulled into his drive.

'You look like shit,' said Ross as he bounded up the stairs, pausing at the threshold to envelop William in a hug.

'Thank you.'

'And you stink of whisky. How long have you been drinking?'

'I don't know,' William answered honestly.

'You can't go on like this.'

They both settled into the two chairs overlooking the harbour, Ross in the one Gill used to occupy.

From the outside, overlooking Victoria Road, the pastel grey-blue exterior was majestically fake Georgian, in a way only the Australians could pull off, fronted by square-shaped box hedges, not a leaf out of place.

The marble-floored interior hall led on the right to handsome, wide stairs to the first, bedroom floor and past them, a panorama opening the further one went into the house: sheets of glass, delicately partitioned and affording extensive views, beyond the pool, from Middle Harbour to the North East and the Harbour Bridge and Opera House to the west. The effect was shimmeringly stunning.

Central to this large expanse of floor covering the entire back of the house, with a kitchen behind to the left and a TV room behind to the right, were two large, comfy chairs, placed in such a way to afford the widest breadth of view possible. A small, mahogany table nestled between them holding a half-full bottle of Lagavulin and a half-empty glass of the same.

'I don't know what else to do.'

'I've been thinking.'

'Oh dear. That sounds ominous.'

'Maybe more than you might imagine.'

'Oh ...?'

'Since I've known you, you've been loved to the hilt by Gill. Before that, you were part of an academic community where all your wants were provided. Right?'

'Well, yes. It was an amenable way of life. Oxford, I mean.'

'In Babylon you were part of a large team. And there was a woman ...'

'Ellie. Ellie Green.'

'That's right.'

They lapsed into a mutual silence.

'Anyway ... you've always had a supportive community about

you and now, when you need it most, that's all changed. You just can't stay cooped up here in this oversized house on your own. And the University of Sydney is certainly not Oriel College, Oxford.'

Silence.

'I'm your closest friend ...' It was true: for the last 18 months, Farnsom had been a stay in his life. Ross, and his wife Anne, had grown attached to William and Gill and guided them exuberantly into life in Sydney, introducing them to new friends (Ross had the most extensive network of friends and acquaintances William had ever encountered. He seemed to know everyone who was anyone in Sydney and beyond, many his patients or family and friends of patients), new experiences (the eclectic offering of the Opera House and the New South Wales Art Gallery were particular pleasures), new places and a general contentment that William would never have dreamed possible. And now, with Gill's death, all that had evaporated.

'... And the last thing I want to do is lose you. But ...'

'Yes?'

'But ... you've got to go back home. There's too much Gill here for you ever to escape this misery.

'I'm the last one to want to see you go. But you need the old certainties to give you a chance to live again ...'

As his voice trailed off into the openness of possibility, William realised the truth of Ross' suggestion: his only hope lay in regressing to a way of life he knew and in which he felt comfortable.

◆ ◆ ◆

They'd decided on the War Memorial Hospital in Waverley for the birth. The Prince of Wales or Saint Vincent's were the obvious choices and all three were roughly equidistant to their home in Bellevue Hill. But the Prince of Wales and Saint Vincent's were too imposing, too impersonal, too monolithic. The War Memorial was more homely: there the nurses would remember your name without having to check the clipboard at the end of the bed first.

Not being sensitive to such considerations, William would have been content with any of the three, but Gill was adamant.

Occasionally, they would detour past the hospital on the way to work at the University of Sydney. And Gill was, the bigger she got, more excited at the prospect of the birth of their baby girl.

William was in the kitchen preparing Gill's light breakfast of tea and toast when she called to him from their bed. It was neither shrill nor panicked but the urgency of her call alarmed William. He left the tray unset and dashed to her side.

Gill had said nothing, merely showed him the small, bright stain on the bed where she'd lain.

She was not yet due; three weeks to go. But was this normal? A harbinger of an imminent labour? Should they call the doctor? Go to the hospital? Neither of them knew, but both wordlessly tried to mask their visceral fear that this was not normal. There had been no suggestions of premature bleeding in the NCT classes and no warning of such a thing from the midwife.

But then Gill had clutched her nightshirt into a bunch between her legs as the pain shot through her right side and a crimson circle formed in the cinched nightie around her hand.

She looked to William, silently begging his help.

'I'll call an ambulance,' he said, dialling 000 as Gill bent over, softly moaning, willing the pain to go and the bleeding to stop.

William breathed the panic back down his chest as Gill complained of the pain spasming across her abdomen.

He sat her gently on the bed as the blood continued to spread the stain on her nightdress.

What might have happened to cause this?

Gill had been careful: no alcohol, only appropriate NCT exercises, gentle walking, healthy diet …

'Which service do you require?'

'Ambulance, please. It's urgent …'

Within 20 minutes Gill was – now sweating and radiating heat – being blue-lighted in the ambulance to the hospital, with William in their car behind, failing to keep up.

When he arrived at the War Memorial Hospital in Birrell Street, there was no sign of the ambulance; no Gill being stretchered to a ward. All seemed calm, even mundane. But the apparent tranquillity only served to exacerbate William's mounting alarm.

He managed to park, ignored the threatening signs demanding payment for the privilege, and ran to reception on the ground floor.

'Please. Where's my wife?' Panic had now set in.

'Your name, sir?'

'Adams. She is Dr Gill Adams.'

A few deft clicks of the keyboard.

'We have no-one of that name here, Mr Adams.'

'But you must. I've just followed the ambulance. She is not well. They were only five minutes ahead of me.'

More clicks.

'I can see that Dr Adams is registered here, Mr Adams, but I'm afraid she's not been admitted. You say she was in an ambulance?'

'Yes.'

Yet more clicks.

'We don't take emergency admissions here. Ah, yes. She's been admitted to Prince of Wales ...'

And before she could finish the sentence, William had turned and ran towards the car.

He crumpled the penalty notice nestled under his windscreen wiper and threw it to the ground.

Parking at the Prince of Wales was even more tortuous. He'd done a circuit of the hospital's forecourt in the hope of spotting the ambulance – there were four parked in the bays set aside for the purpose – and had then to drive back down the entrance ramp, wait for what seemed like eternity to snake his place into the queue at the roundabout, turn back up the entrance ramp and then divert left down into the underground car park.

There were no places on his endless circuit of the basement level. But he managed to find one at the furthest remove from the lifts on Basement 2. He grabbed the suitcase they'd packed for Gill's hospital stay the month before and headed for the lifts.

Which seemed wilfully to ignore him, the stairs hid from him and, once the lift arrived, it deliberately slowed its pace before disgorging him on the ground floor.

Immediately opposite the opening lift was the Information Desk, a smiling attendant dispensing with her last enquirer just as he arrived, still breathing heavily from his dash from the car to the obdurate lift.

'Obstetrics, please,' he wheezed.

'Obstetrics and Gynaecology is on the third floor, Sir,' she smiled, 'Just turn left ...'

But before she could finish, he'd rushed back to do battle with the lifts.

When eventually he found his way to reception at Obstetrics and Gynaecology, he found that Gill was not there.

'She's been admitted to Intensive Care, Sir. Ninth floor.'

Distraught, William made his way back to the lifts, still

clutching Gill's case.

The receptionist at Intensive Care invited him to take a seat in the empty waiting area. Two two-seater sofas in muted beige were wedged on either side of a coffee machine which sat on a corner console sporting plastic cups, milk capsules, spoons and sugar sachets. The walls were painted a soothing cream and held anodyne landscapes in identikit frames. All was calm. William sat, beside himself.

His heart strained to burst from his chest as he leaned his elbows onto his knees, buried his face in his hands, and heaved great sobs of uncontrolled anguish.

Seeing his distress, the receptionist came and sat next to him.

'I'm sure it's nothing to worry about,' she assured him. She clearly had no knowledge yet of what they were doing with Gill. 'They're always exceptionally cautious here.' And when he didn't respond, 'Someone will be with you as soon as they have any news.' She patted him on the arm and returned to her desk.

After half an hour, a doctor in blue scrubs, his long, mousey-coloured hair in a net, approached William from the double doors sealing the way to the unit which William assumed housed Gill.

'Mr Adams?'

'Yes,' said William, rising, to take the proffered hand.

'Please, sit down. I'm sorry to have kept you waiting, but we have some complications. Just to be on the safe side, we're going to keep Gill in for a couple of days for precautions ...'

'But what's wrong? Can I see her? I ...'

The doctor, Mr Gilson – clearly a surgeon, William dimly registered – put his hand gently on William's shoulder.

'We're not exactly sure what's happening,' he said 'but we should have a pretty good idea tonight, by the time we get the results of the blood tests.

'But Gill is stable. We're reducing her blood pressure, which was abnormally high. The bleeding has stopped and mother and baby's vitals are all within acceptable limits.'

William took no comfort in Gilson's prattle; his words all seemed to shout trouble: *complications, on the safe side, precautions, blood tests, abnormally high, vitals.* They screamed danger to him.

Gilson's soothing words, his gentle demeanour, confirmed in William's mind that whatever it was that Gill was suffering, it was desperately serious. Gilson suggested that William should go home. He could not see Gill in her present, heavily sedated, state. He might like to pack a bag – clearly Gilson hadn't noticed the bag sitting between William's legs – and they would ring him the moment they had anything to report. But William was right to have called an ambulance and everything was going to be fine.

He'd said this gently, caringly, professionally. William knew that he'd said just that one thousand times before and doubtless, on occasion, what he'd said was true.

But equally William knew that he simply couldn't know that everything was going to be fine.

◆ ◆ ◆

Once home, William had the wits to call Elkin, his and Gill's Head of Department at the University, and tell him what had happened. He also left a message with Adrienne, Ross Farnsom's PA.

The night drive to the Prince of Wales was dismal. The skies blackened then sharply shed torrential rain, drumming the roof of his car and mirroring the tears that ran down his cheeks.

William darted from the lift as it reached the ninth floor and was greeted by that morning's receptionist, now clearly alert to his plight. There was no change to Gill's condition but at least he could see her now.

The aircon in the reception area was chilly but as they pressed through the double doors, into Intensive Care proper, the temperature rose to a comfortable ambience.

She took him past medical staff working a line of curtained cubicles and then to individual rooms smelling astringently clinical.

Gill's room was the second last on the left before the dead end of the corridor. The lights of the room were off but a bank of machinery, for monitoring purposes William guessed, shed a surreal, contrived glow over the figure of Gill, huddled under light blue sheets.

The receptionist ushered William in, noting that Gill had been sedated, before she left him alone, retracing her steps.

William sat in the red plastic bucket chair at her side. He reached for her hand, resisting the need to hold it tight, and willing her to respond. Even in some tiny way: pressure on his own hand, a fluttering eyelid, a noise; anything to acknowledge his presence and his deep love for her.

But her breathing remained steady, her eyes closed, and her hand unresponsive.

Two hours later, as he trudged into the reception area, his thoughts a whirl of mystified, uninformed alarm, he was greeted, as he was about to enter the lift, by Mr Gilson, who sat him down in the still empty sofa.

'The blood tests show a deterioration in Gill's immune system,' he said, after reassuring blandishments. 'There is a chemical imbalance ... placental ... possibly pre-eclampsia ... viability ... hypertensive ...'

The words floated in and out of William's consciousness. And try as he may, battling bone-weary mental and emotional exhaustion, he could seem to do little to register just what it was that Gill was suffering.

'Thrombosis is not uncommon,' said Gilson, 'and there is always the possibility of sepsis due to pregnancy-related infection, but we're pretty confident that neither is what Gill is suffering …'

The words the surgeon used seemed like judgements: in spite of his bland assurances that 'there is nothing to worry about' and that Gill would be kept 'for a few days' observation', 'merely as a precaution', William felt anything but assured.

◆ ◆ ◆

The next day, as he arrived early, a nurse at reception informed him that Gill had had a comfortable night.

'She was awake just now. Would you like to see her?'

Dare he hope that Gill had turned a corner? That last night's horrors and his accumulated fears had dissipated with the morning mists?

He opened her door, only to be greeted by a smiling Gill, her arms spread wide to embrace.

He gladly held her.

But at the same time, he felt the feebleness of her hug; her coolness, so unlike the fire she gave off in the depth of her illness; her weakness.

'My love!'

'I was worried about you.' It sounded so banal but it gave at least a shallow voice to his deepest fear.

'I'm feeling much better.'

'Thank God.'

'You don't believe in God.'

'Maybe. But I thank Him, anyway. So, tell me truly: are you really feeling better?'

'Well, I'm exhausted to be honest …'

'What about the pain ... and the bleeding?'

'The bleeding's stopped ... and the pain, well, that's intermittent. And apart from feeling very tired, I'm much better.'

'I'm so happy.'

Then taking her arms gently in both hands and holding her at arms' length, the better to look into her eyes, he continued to hold her. 'But have you seen Mr Gilson? What does he say?'

'I'm not really sure. They've had me sedated. He was here when I woke up but I'm not certain what he said, except that he was sure I'll be fine.' She shrugged.

William was not sure whether Gill was any more convinced than he was but he took her in his arms again to reassure her of his undying love.

It was not long before his embrace was so limply returned that he realised she'd fallen asleep. At least now her breathing was regular, even strong. And she'd lost the clamminess of last night.

By lunchtime, while Gill still slept, a passing nurse encouraged William to take a rest or at least to go and eat. 'She'll be fine,' she assured him.

It was later that afternoon that William returned. The two nurses at the nurses' station within the unit were deep in conversation as he passed but both offered him encouraging smiles.

Although light outside, the shades of her room had been drawn and in the dim light of the machine bank by her bed, Gill slept, her legs raised, her belly bulge resplendent. William even thought he detected a smile in the gentle upturn at the corners of her lips.

He touched her forehead lightly. The heat of the night before had, indeed, gone but she was still coated in a light patina of sweat, limning her dark features, giving her black face a ghostly sheen.

He held her unresponsive hand.

He placed his hand on her bump, and just as he was about to withdraw it, he felt a response from within. His daughter moved, as if in answer to his touch. Again, the tears which had flowed so freely this last day came to his eyes, unbidden save for the knowledge that his child had spoken to him.

He pulled the chair near to the bed, laid his head beside Gill's hand, and joined her in sleep.

He was disorientated when he awoke; it took time to place himself in the right continent, such had been his tangled dreams, with the woman he loved, by her side.

He marvelled at her sleeping beauty, the sparkle of her jet black curls, the slope of her thick eyelashes, the wide symmetry of her face. He couldn't resist placing a gentle kiss on those eminently kissable lips, now slightly apart in repose.

In spite of his long sleep at her side, exhaustion pulsed through his body in waves. He decided to go home to rest. No point being so tired as to be of no use to Gill when she recovered.

On his retreat, he learnt at the nurses' station that Ross and Anne Farnsom and Anthony Elkin and his wife had all visited that afternoon while he and Gill both slept.

And before he finished his shift, Mr Gilson had stopped by to say that he was happy with Gill's progress: although her blood pressure remained a touch high, her other vitals were fine; she'd had no further pains and the bleeding had stopped completely. Another full day, maybe two, and she could go home.

Gill was getting better.

When he arrived the following morning, Gill was tucking into a generous breakfast: juice, fruit, followed by eggs, bacon and toast and a large cup of black coffee. It was just the best news.

The hours that followed had by now become something of a blur in William's mind: that afternoon, they'd sat nattering, Gill eating prodigiously, the both of them laughing, sharing the taste of favoured girl's names on their tongues.

The following day, he'd woken early, bought their favourite breakfast at the Boatshed Cafe at Double Bay and shared it with her as they both sat on her bed, their legs slung over the side, dangling over the glossy linoleum floor.

'I've been thinking,' said Gill, 'my mother's name was Jenymungup; it means *plenty of gum* …'

William was puzzled.

'As in gum trees, you ass,' she joked.

'Oh …'

'I think I'd like to call her after my mother.'

'You want to call her Jenygungup?'

'It's Jenymungup. And no, I wouldn't saddle any child with that particular mouthful. At least not these days and in our particular circumstances. Although I do think it's a pretty name.'

'Yes?'

'I was thinking Jeny …'

'You don't think Jennifer?'

'No. I specifically don't want to anglicize it. I want it to speak of my mother. To give our girl a rootedness.' She looked at William, just a little nervously. This mattered to Gill, and William, more than most, was aware of the importance of names.

'It *is* a pretty name. I like it.'

'So Jeny it is,' Gill confirmed.

'Jeny it is,' he agreed, savouring the name of his soon-to-be-born daughter on his tongue.

❖ ❖ ❖

Everything was quiet that evening. The visitors had gone, as had Mr Gilson. The new shift of nurses had arrived and routinely made their way between the quiet susurrus of machinery monitoring and, in some cases, maintaining the lives of those sequestered in the gentle, reassuring corridors of the ninth floor.

Gill was asleep and William was contemplating an early night. But as he reached for her hand, her fingers formed a fist and spasms shook her arms. Her whole body began to twist and writhe; her back arched; her teeth clenched and through them came an eviscerating wrench of pain.

William fumbled for the call button, pressed it, repeatedly, was just about to dash to the nurses' station when two came rushing through the door, pushing him gently aside, their urgent ministrations unspoken but hurried. Gill was moved to her side, facing away from William.

It was then that he saw the pool of blood spreading across the sheet beneath her, flushing, flooding out of her.

Gilson was called from wherever he'd been; he must have been within the hospital as he arrived within minutes.

Within seconds of his arrival, Gill was being, at his command, wheeled into theatre.

William was left standing aghast, his eyes fixed on the bloodstained bed. More alone than he'd been in his life, as Gill was led to her fate.

It was still standing thus that they found him half an hour later.

Although Gilson spoke soothing, quiet, gentle words, none seemed to register in William's mind.

He was led to another room, he knew not where, and there, on a gurney, covered in a green operating sheet, was Gill.

They seemed to recede from his senses as he moved forward to lift the sheet to reveal the woman he longed to live.

But here was Gill: still, at rest, gone.

◆ ◆ ◆

In the space of a few months, William sold his Bellevue Hill mansion with its five bedrooms, harbour views and pool. He left his job at Sydney University. He farewelled his friends, particularly the Farnsoms and the Elkins.

He wept over the shoreline rocks by Bear Island at La Perouse where Gill's and his daughter's - Jeny's - ashes had been scattered.

And he returned to England.

He forewent blue skies, unremitting warmth, at times sapping humidity, and a pearlescent tinge that coloured everything: trees, rocks, buildings, birds, even people.

And he walked into a world hued grey, in the January-middle of an Oxford winter.

CHAPTER 2

Claire, William's erstwhile PA, snapped at the offer of her old job back. She had, for almost all his time at Oxford, organised his daily life, paid his bills, booked his holidays and ensured that all his days ran smoothly.

Officially, she had retired when he'd left for Australia almost two years before. But she'd found retirement unfulfilling, boring. Bridge at the Oxford Bridge Club in Summertown was simply not enough. Nor had she enjoyed the skimping she had to make without the generous remuneration William provided.

His wealth, rumoured to be approaching one billion, was legendary in Oxford. It was inherited from his widowed, industrialist father who'd died when William was 21. Fortunately, his fortunes were managed by a staid city firm of 'wealth managers' so Claire's responsibilities were not particularly onerous. And now she had her old job – and handsome salary – back. At 56, she was happy again, and still quietly in love with the much younger William, utterly oblivious to her affection for him.

After lunch at The Ivy in The High with a still jetlagged William, she'd skipped across the street to the Covered Market for a second coffee to celebrate her reappointment before catching a taxi to her flat in Summertown. They'd renewed text, email and WhatsApp numbers and he'd handed over his diary, such as it was, for her to manage.

William received hundreds of letters a month inviting him to speak at universities, think tanks, clubs and institutions; asking him to be patron, president or adviser. He also, given his wealth, got just as many missives asking for donations or sponsorship or support. All of these he ignored. It would now be Claire's job to sift through the morass of requests, sorting the wheat from the chaff, 90 percent of which she would discard without even opening. The redirection of William's mail was a blessing for the College porters and a nightmare for Claire's Summertown postman.

She knew this meant that, although they'd communicate frequently, she'd seldom see him, as had been the case before he'd left for his sabbatical in Sydney where he'd found love... and death... And had become the somewhat isolated and distracted man she'd been saddened to become reacquainted with. Daily she would message him his commitments and appointments, occasionally nudging him with gentle reminders, jealously guarding his privacy from those who would distract him.

Once back in her flat, she set about organising his daily round, considering holiday destinations, ensuring that all his other personal properties dotted around England and France were secure and in good shape. She checked with Nonna Claudia that his apartment in Venice was ready for occupation. Although they'd not discussed it, she was sure that he'd wish to return to Dorsoduro, the arty suburb in Venice where his apartment was, soon, even if only for a weekend. At least, that was how the old William would play things.

Claire rang her would-be suitor, Rupert, ever ready to do her bidding, to arrange a meal that evening. And she looked forward to the inevitable fuck afterwards.

◆ ◆ ◆

William was surprised that the soon-to-retire Provost of Oriel College, Oxford had, without being asked, arranged for him to occupy his old rooms, the former chaplain's digs in Front Quad.

More surprising was that the Provost informed him, upon his arrival in Oriel, of the ground-swell among the Fellows for William to be appointed the new Provost to succeed him.

The Times had dubbed William 'the world's most famous archaeologist', a soubriquet that had stuck. He'd earned the title after months in the desert sands of Iraq where he'd helped oversee the excavation of the Nabopolassar Archive under the great library of King Nebuchadnezzar of Babylon.

Find after spectacular find had revealed hitherto unknown secrets about the ancient world that had captured the imagination of the public who longed for the romance and derring-do of the intrepid team of academics who had braved life and limb to reveal hidden truths about the past. At least that was the way the cliché-ridden *Times* portrayed it.

In truth, the British Museum expedition of scholars slogged relentlessly in the Iraqi heat to unearth undreamt-of treasures from the unforgiving soil of ancient Babylon. There William had worked, and fallen in love with, Professor Ellie Green. He'd translated an old Sumerian cylinder – a previously unknown recension of the Gilgamesh Epic – and in so doing had opened a Pandora's box which brought into question the religious rationale behind the land boundaries of the combustible Middle East.

More importantly, from William's point of view as a scholar of Egyptology, he'd deciphered a stela written in Meroitic, an untranslated language of the ancient Kingdom of Nubia – or Kush, as it was known in the Bible – written in Egyptian script. It was a colossal achievement turning William into a modern-day Rosetta stone-deciphering Champollion.

The dig, and its many momentous finds, had been interrupted

by a deadly attack by agents of ISIS. After a return to London, where William and Ellie's lives were threatened, the resumed dig revealed more treasures until it was finally closed down after a full-scale assault on the site by ISIS which decimated the British Museum team.

All of this, together with William's burgeoning relationship with Ellie, was recounted in breathless encomiums by 'embedded' reporters who played it to the hilt for a parched public thirsty for every detail of spectacular finds, biblical history, and love among the desert dunes.

For a brief while, William and Ellie were the world's most famous, and adored, couple. When the excavation was formally ended, Ellie had declined William's proposal of marriage, knowing full well that a transatlantic relationship – she returned to a professorship at Harvard – would never work and that neither of them could bear to live outside their native countries (a decision she came later to regret – after an extremely brief and very unsatisfactory marriage – but about which William never knew).

On his return to England, William found himself thrust into a limelight he hated, followed and courted by a press he despised. He craved the anonymity he had enjoyed, despite his riches, prior to his Babylonian excursion.

It was as much to escape the press, and the devastation of Ellie's refusal of his proposal, as anything else that he'd accepted the offer from the University of Sydney of a Visiting Professorship in the Department of Archaeology that same year as his return to England.

His hopes of a quiet life, however, were demolished when a random discovery in the Australian outback led to even greater press exposure: a chance find in caves near the Northern Territory town of Birdum of the only example of Aboriginal writing led to William and Anthony Elkin, Professor of Archaeology at the University of Sydney and William's nominal boss, together with a delegation from the Northern Territory government in Darwin, to investigate the site.

It was there that William met Dr Gill Reed with whom he fell in love. Between them, they managed to decipher the script. But unbeknownst to them, the machinations of both Federal Government and an unscrupulous, acquisitive American mining company intent on exploiting the site for its vast reserves of uranium, led to Gill's abduction and rape.

After she was found, the developing relationship led to her marriage with William, their settling into his newly-acquired home in Bellevue Hill in Sydney and her pregnancy, which in turn led to her death.

William's earlier fame ensured that this new discovery and translation of Aboriginal writing compounded his celebrity rendering them both household names in Australia, famous internationally and lauded in academia, particularly for William as the only man ever to decipher two un-cracked, and completely separate, languages.

Sadly, the press interest, little short of voyeurism, continued with Gill's pregnancy and death.

All of this was related by *The Mail* reporter, Sam Wilson, who'd first run the daily column on *The Babylonian Treasure Trove*, now transmogrified into *The Aboriginal Mystery Script* and finally into the tragedy of Gill's death and William's despair.

Inevitably, William's friends and acquaintances in Oxford had thus kept abreast of his life in a way they knew he must have resented.

It was all this fame, coupled with his unrivalled discoveries and undoubted erudition, that led to a popular groundswell amongst the Fellows of Oriel College for his appointment as the new Provost, the Head of College.

This development too was reported in the press, together with leaked voices of opposition to William's nomination, making a sensation out of a non-story: William neither welcomed nor wanted the Provostship. He had refused it when the outgoing Provost had first informed him of support for his appointment to the post and he would refuse it still, under all circumstances.

What he did not decline was the Chair of Regius Professor of Egyptology, bestowed by the new King, who had quietly followed William's comings and goings with great interest. It was the first Regius Professorship created in 200 years and an honour William humbly accepted.

Although he couldn't see the end of it, William knew in his bones that the interest surrounding his professional life and the tragedy of Gill's death would soon subside. But he desperately wanted his privacy to be afforded soon and his cherished anonymity to be restored.

It seemed that most support for the 'opposition' candidate for Provost was coalescing around Hamish Grant, a Professorial Fellow in Linguistics at Oriel.

William had known Grant since he first arrived in Oxford and had always disliked him. Not only was he the sort of person who always looked over your shoulder when he spoke with you to see if there was someone more important in the room who better deserved his attention, he was undilutedly snide and cynical: contemptuous of everything that provided him not only with his livelihood but of the pampered and sumptuous surroundings that made his life so apparently easy, yet which he carped about so cravenly.

It rankled with William that they'd ended up sitting next to each other that week on high table.

'What a pleasure to have you back,' Grant had lied, looking over the top of his glasses which hung on a gold chain around his neck.

'It's good to be back home,' William said, without much feeling.

'I hear there's a move to make you Provost.'

'I have no interest in the job.'

'That's not what I hear. The Fellows are positively bursting with enthusiasm at the prospect of having such a famous fellow to lead them.'

William's distress at readjusting to life in Oxford without Gill was more than enough to justify a pointed riposte but, one way or another, he'd have to live with this pompous creep. Besides, Gill's direct, if gentle, honesty had taught him a lesson for life.

'Hamish, I have no interest in the job. I will never accept it. I will not even oppose it being offered to you, in spite of your feigned indifference to it, or to anything that is important, for that matter.

'Now if you'll excuse me ...' And with that William rose, nodded in the direction of the Provost, seated two along and who must at least have half-heard the conversation, and left the dining hall.

It was not long after that that the not unsensitive Fellows realised William had no interest in becoming Provost and turned their attention to other candidates, including Hamish Grant, although most still hoped for William's appointment, in spite of his uninterest.

CHAPTER 3

The phone call from Prof Andy Verity at Princeton University had been an awkward one. Andy was Prof Dominic Taylor's brother-in-law and William had met him, only once, at Dom's funeral.

Dom was the Director of the British Museum team of archaeologists at the dig in ancient Babylon. It was Dom who had rung William, the night after his girlfriend Robin had stormed out on him on their seventh date at The Bear and Ragged Staff in Cumnor, a gastropub just outside Oxford. That incident, together with a debilitating asthma attack and a general sense of helplessness, had led William, against inclination and common sense, to allow himself to be cajoled into joining the dig the following day. And the rest, of course, was history: it was Dom's invitation that had led to William's translation of the Cylinder of Babylon and, more importantly from William's academic point of view, to cracking the code of the undeciphered language of Meroitic.

While on the dig, William and Ellie had become close friends with Dom. And his death, by suicide, had affected them deeply.

After his death, suspended by the neck from a rope tied to the top of a bell tent at the dig site, his body was removed to England where the funeral was held and William and Ellie had met Andy and his wife, Dom's sister, Kathleen.

Dom had been instrumental in bringing Andy and Kathleen

together thirty years before and they now had an only son, Larry, who was twenty-two.

It was about Larry that Andy had rung William.

Larry Verity had graduated from his father's Ivy League university, Princeton, New Jersey, *summa cum laude*, the equivalent of a first class degree. It was largely due to his uncle Dom's influence that Larry had studied Egyptology at Princeton. And now he wanted to complete a doctorate and since William and Dom had been such good friends, and following William's earth-shattering discoveries and achievements, Andy wanted William to be Larry's supervisor for his D.Phil at Oxford. It was the best possible career move he could make.

William was devastated. He'd vowed, years before and after the murder of his doctoral student Jeremy White, never to supervise a doctorate again. More particularly, he didn't need to: as a multi-millionaire, he drew no salary from the University; indeed, he was a generous, though anonymous, donor to Oriel College. He was at liberty, academically speaking, to do pretty much as he liked. And at present, that meant completing his longstanding and painstaking work on his *Meroitic Lexicon*, essentially a dictionary of all known Meroitic words, referenced to ancient texts and cross-referenced to other ancient languages, much in the manner of Liddell and Scott's *Greek Lexicon,* one of the greatest intellectual achievements of the late nineteenth century. In that time, it had been impossible in England to be any further than three miles from someone who could read ancient Greek, in that every parish priest in the land had at least a smattering of it and not long before that, every graduate of Oxford had to be in holy orders where Greek was a graduation requirement. William had always been an admirer of Dean Scott.

Scott had been Dean of Rochester Cathedral from 1870-1887. During this time, along with Liddell, they had spent most of their waking hours poring over ancient Greek and Latin texts researching their *Lexicon*. William quite liked the fact that, while he was supposed to be running a Cathedral, whose Bishop's house was Lambeth Palace in London, he was actually beavering away at his academic research leaving the maintenance of the cathedral and its worship entirely to others. While not necessarily hoping to emulate Scott, William did admire his single-mindedness in working on an achievement that would long outlast him. Indeed, Liddell and Scott, as their *Lexicon* is always known, remains the standard reference work in the field, even after such a long time. William hoped for something not dissimilar for his own *Lexicon*.

But William's connection with Rochester had been greater than that. Four years before, William and his then girlfriend Laura had attempted to solve the mystery of Laura's boyfriend's, Jeremy White's, death and their researches had taken them to Rochester Cathedral where Laura had been educated at The King's School. In the course of their investigations, they had made some remarkable discoveries and William had come to learn more about, and to admire, Scott.

And now Andy Verity was asking William to break his own rules in taking on his son for three or four years of study which could only serve to distract from his own work on the *Lexicon*. Something Scott would never have countenanced.

And yet, he did owe much to Dom. Were it not for Dom he would never have been able to translate the Cylinder of Babylon. Were it not for Dom, he would never have cracked Meroitic; these two were his greatest intellectual achievements. And, more importantly, Dom was his friend. And Andy was, he knew, playing on that friendship to ask a very big favour.

Doubtless, Andy was unaware of the fact that William drew no salary and therefore did not have the same obligations as other academics; doubtless he was unaware of William's steadfast rule not to take on doctoral students; doubtless he was unaware of just what an imposition he was making. Yet ask he did. And William was seriously conflicted.

In the end, he felt he couldn't refuse, for Dom's sake, and tried to convince himself that supervising a doctorate would not be too much of a distraction.

The one bright spot in this sorry saga was that Andy had informed William that Larry proposed, for his thesis, *Evidence of the Introduction of the Rebus Principle in the Development of Meroitic.* Such research would be an invaluable resource for scholars of Meroitic in the future. If it were successful. But William simply could not see, given that the understanding of Meroitic was so nascent, just how the introduction of Rebus could be identified. He was both intrigued and mystified.

◆ ◆ ◆

It did not take long before William settled into the daily round with which he was previously so familiar, eased as it was by Claire's ministrations.

He lectured once a week. He refused the many requests he received from all over the world from students to be supervised in their post-graduate work by him. He ignored the growing number of letters from scholars wanting to develop his ideas, to collaborate with him, to show him the errors of his academic ways … He read. He wrote. He fell into the regulated pattern dictated by College life. But all this hardly managed to dull the grief he carried of Gill's death. It was not uncommon, indeed it was becoming a habit, that he would weep himself to sleep after drinking too much whisky. His grief, or was it the winter weather of the Oxford bowl, exacerbated his asthma. It seemed he wheezed for hours on end these cold, miserable days.

◆ ◆ ◆

The most prestigious global centre for Egyptian studies was

the Taylor Institute, abutting the world's oldest museum, the Ashmolean.

Although, with the wane of interest in all things ancient, the Taylorian, as it was known, was now interested principally in the study of the languages of Europe, it retained, at its heart, a core of world-beating scholarly interest in all things ancient Egyptian.

Established in 1845, and funded from the estate of the architect Sir Robert Taylor, it occupied the east wing of the neo-classical building of the Ashmolean, subsequently extended and restored, in St Giles, in the heart of Oxford. . It was here that Sir Flinders Petrie, with no formal education, discoverer of the Merneptah Stele and of Proto-Sinaitic script, expositor of Tanis, held the first Chair of Egyptology in the UK. And here that Sir Alan Gardiner, Fellow of Queen's College, advisor to Lord Carnarvon and Howard Carter on the translation of writing on objects found in Tutankhamun's tomb, wrote his famous *Egyptian Grammar*, still the standard text for learning Middle Kingdom hieroglyphs. It was here that the Egypt Exploration Society, which oversaw the discovery, among other things, of the mortuary temple of Hatshepsut, was based.

The Taylor Institute's director, James Southwell, had known William as an undergraduate and, as an Egyptologist himself, had followed William's career with interest. A mutual benefit accrued to both the Institute and to William himself that Southwell had arranged for William to occupy a spacious office in the Institute but also to be appointed Senior Fellow there. The post was little more than ceremonial. But it afforded William direct access to the world's greatest collection of Egyptian research materials and brought much kudos to the Institute itself.

The world-class staff of over forty professors, researchers and students provided William with an unrivalled resource for his own work in completing his *Lexicon* of Meroitic.

His work on the *Lexicon* had – understandably – fallen into abeyance during his time in Australia. And returning to it, in this most amenable of settings, was one of the few pleasures he enjoyed since Gill's death.

Southwell had arranged all the staff into parallel lines in the main library to greet William as he took up his Fellowship. All four walls of the library were covered, floor to ceiling, in ancient tomes, giving the room a feeling which pulsed with arcane knowledge. It was all rather embarrassing and reminded William of something out of *Downton Abbey*.

James was meticulous in introducing each colleague by title, name and job description before appending a brief résumé of what it was they were currently working on.

Inevitably, this was taking an age and William was only too conscious of keeping all these people away from their jobs just so that they might meet or be reacquainted with him.

But everyone was delightful and none seemed impatient to be getting back to work. All things Egyptian had a timeless quality about them, it seemed.

William was nervous that he would forget so many of their names and details and felt awkward being the centre of attention. Indeed, several of the women showed him rather more attention than he felt comfortable with.

In an earlier life, he'd always battled with the interest that women had shown in him. He was not vain enough to believe he was so overwhelmingly attractive that women had to fall at his feet, and so he cynically assumed that, for many, his great wealth must form probably the major part of that attraction.

By 38, he'd loved four women: Laura, Ellie, Robin and Gill. Laura and Ellie had refused him; Robin he'd alienated, and Gill had died.

He was overwhelmingly unlucky in love and, with the complicating factor of his riches, he was unconfident about where any relationship might take him.

He'd just met Jill Flinders... another Gill, and he was starting to flag emotionally and physically. He wished for it to end, to go to his office, close the door, drink a generous whisky and go back to the letter *Mêm*, in his *Lexicon*.

'And this is Dr Jack Sutherland,' said James, 'he's our expert on the history of Napatan and Meroë, but he has a particular personal interest...'

'It's only a hobby, really, if you're going to say what I think you are,' said Jack smiling, '... in Tuthmosis III.'

'Of course, I know Dr Sutherland's work,' said William shaking his hand enthusiastically. 'I thought your recent paper on economic expansion in Nubia and beyond in the reign of Taharqa in *The Journal of Egyptian Studies* was outstanding.'

'Why, thank you!'

Sutherland was short, wiry and possessed of an enormous forehead on which sat a mop of tousled, thick hair, like a crumpled rug. He sported thick, black-rimmed glasses which made his eyes look impossibly and disconcertingly large.

'I'd be very grateful if I could pick your brains for my *Lexicon* at some point,' said William.

'I would be delighted.'

William was glad to have made Sutherland's acquaintance. He was surprised they'd not met before. The circle of Egyptologists in Oxford, while world-renown, was not large. But a shared interest in things Meroitic was bound to cement their future together.

'I look forward to working with you.'

'And this is Dr Mira Pelushkaya...'

◆ ◆ ◆

The highlight of William's week was his trip, on Wednesdays, to London. The train from Oxford Parkway to Marylebone took an hour.

Claire organised William's driver to take him to the station and return him to Oriel the following day in time for College lunch. In London, he resumed his practice of training all afternoon at his Soho *dojo* – he was a black belt, second dan in *Shorinji Kempo*, a Japanese form of *Shaolin Kung Fu* – before retiring to his club, the Athenaeum, in Pall Mall. There he would shower, change into a suit, have his evening meal, invariably at the club table, and retire to the room – always Number 14 – Claire had reserved for him.

William's weekly visits to the Athenaeum were not without regret: his most poignant memory of the Club was the night after Robin had stormed out on him on their seventh date, citing his inability to commit as the reason.

The following night, after his lecture to a small group of club members on Meroitic, and in the throes of one of the most debilitating asthma attacks he could remember, he'd received the phone call from Dominic Taylor inviting him to the British Museum archaeological dig in the ancient city of Babylon. The following day he was there: he'd met Dom, met Ellie Green, and started work on the Cylinder of Babylon, as it became known.

That decision to go had changed his life forever: it thrust upon him an unwanted fame consequent upon his translation of the Cylinder and his deciphering the language of Meroitic after the discovery of what came later to be known as the Adams Stela. He'd fallen in love with Ellie who had refused his offer of marriage, which in turn led to his decision to take a sabbatical in Australia where he'd met Gill who was now lost to him, equally forever.

Try as he might, he was unable to expunge this chain of memory every time he visited the Club; it formed a fug of unwelcome thoughts and feelings each time he wafted into sleep in Room 14.

Nonetheless, as far as he could, he used this weekly interlude to recharge his batteries, both physically and mentally. On Wednesdays, he forewent intellectual activity, read crime fiction on the train and in bed at the Club – GK Galbraith, Mick Herron, Elizabeth George. In Australia, he'd developed a taste for outback *noir* – Chris Hammer, Jane Harper, Garry Disher. But all that was too painful to read now.

These excursions to London helped restore his anonymity, and the settled routine – so much a part of his life before Australia – provided him with an equilibrium he would not have imagined possible only months before, as he cried himself to sleep in his rooms in Oriel.

College life had always been so public but here, on Wednesdays, his privacy was, if not guaranteed, at least enhanced.

CHAPTER 4

William regretted his churlishness at his hesitating over Andy's request that his son, Larry, might undertake his doctorate under William's tutelage. Dom had been a good friend and was in part responsible for William's greatest academic achievements.

He'd sent his driver, Rick, to pick Larry up from Heathrow and then deposit him in the generous, furnished apartment his parents had arranged for him in Oxford, not far from the College.

It was just after College lunch and William was making his way back to his rooms when Rick caught up with him and introduced him to the recently arrived Larry.

Larry was tall and handsome in a waspish kind of way: short buzz haircut, piercing ice blue eyes, set lantern jaw; he was almost something of a caricature. If he'd sported a cardigan with a large P on one side, the picture would have been complete. The overall impression William got was that this man was *neat*.

It was William's practice, after College lunch always accompanied by half a bottle of claret, to retire to his rooms, there to have his 'afternoon kip'. He was not a man who liked his routine interrupted, but again chided himself that he was feeling less than gracious towards his new student.

He invited Larry to his rooms where, after light chitchat about his journey from New York and adjustment to an Oxford winter, they could discuss Larry's proposal for his doctorate.

'I have to confess,' said William, 'that I am intrigued by your proposal to look at the introduction of Rebus in Meroitic.'

The Rebus Principle is the use of existing symbols - in Ancient Egyptian, pictograms - purely for their sounds regardless of meaning, to represent new words. For example, the stylized drawing of three wavy lines, one above the next, in Ancient Egyptian represented 'water', pronounced *nwy*. Over time, the pictogram which stood for water came to mean nothing more than the first sound of the word, in this case the letter *n*.

'Oh, yes?'

'Well,' said William, 'given that Rebus entails identifying a symbol in pictographic script that represents a sound, rather than the item the writer wished to represent, how on earth, in a language – Meroitic – which has only just been deciphered, where there is, as yet, no lexicon, where there are so few examples of the writing … How on earth do you intend to be able to identify something as nuanced as Rebus?'

'I don't know.'

'What?!'

'Look … to be honest, it was my father who suggested that line of research. Don't get me wrong. My Egyptian is quite good. And I've read everything you've written. And I know that extracting Rebus out of as little of Meroitic as we've got is nigh on impossible. And I know that you are half way through your *Lexicon* and that that will be vital in identifying any evidence of Rebus. But I think it's worth at least a try … And I'm sure my uncle Dom would have approved.'

William was both impressed and appalled. The boy clearly had balls, and had been honest enough to confess his father's involvement. But this was potentially an extremely expensive wild goose chase based on so little evidence. And to evince Dom's approval was little short of offensive. Apparently, like father, like son ...

William began to wonder whether Andy's motives in sending his son to Oxford were as honest as he'd suggested.

They finished their meeting with William suggesting that Larry might like to consider the evidence of the introduction of the Rebus principle in well-established translations of ancient languages. In particular, he suggested that Larry should look at translational difficulties in the Gilgamesh Epic. Although written in cuneiform, rather than hieroglyphs, the number of texts discovered was vast and Rebus had been well-established here.

He would see Larry once a fortnight and would expect a 2,500-word paper on agreed subjects. In the meantime, he would ask one or two other post-graduate students to make contact with Larry and to help him settle in.

William felt extremely uneasy both at Larry's proposal and at his admission that his father had misled him, relying as he did on William's moral obligation to Dom's memory.

Already, he was beginning to regret having agreed to Andy's request.

CHAPTER 5

The three-bedroom apartment was no more than a mile away from the Observatory Quarter on the Woodstock Road. A large Victorian house had been converted into four substantial flats, his being on the ground floor, right hand side.

It was decorated meticulously, expensively and spotlessly maintained. The walls were covered in muted abstract paintings which all appeared as if they could just as easily be hung upside down without diminishing the artistic impact.

The drawing room contained no television but sported a wall half of books, half sound system, all built around a large, rectangular painting, hung over a fireplace, that might have been a de Kooning were it not for its monochrome hue. The effect was disconcerting.

The kitchen was impeccable: all marble and granite but with no implements in sight and a feeling of sterility that suggested wrongly that no food was ever cooked there.

The guest bedroom was unused, and five-star hotel-like: tasteful, comfortable and anodyne.

His bedroom was large with windows that overlooked the back of the house. Curtains, however, permanently obscured the view of the neatly maintained, shared garden. A large screen occupied the wall opposite the king-sized bed and by it, shelf upon shelf of pornographic DVDs, not a single one featuring women and many with barely-of-age boys.

Bedside chests had drawers containing paraphernalia whose use could only be guessed at: mechanical and electrical devices of an ingenuity wasted in an occupation of ultimately unsatisfying ends. This was not a room of comfortable dreams and innocent sleep, but its presence was tightly contained: it did not reach beyond the bedroom door into the rest of the apartment, except possibly, the third bedroom, or study, as he preferred to call it.

The study was the only room within the apartment which was permanently locked. Indeed, it was unusual in that it sported a thumb print recognition digital lock, sunk laterally into the right-hand door frame and therefore not obvious to any visitor. Not that there were any visitors.

The study contained a generous desk, a comfortable chair, and an abundance of writing materials. On the desk, sat a large, wraparound computer screen and keyboard.

The walls were covered, floor-to-ceiling, every inch with books: hard-backed, arcane, academic; many in foreign languages, ancient and modern. This was a library, maintained in pristine condition, of a man of monumental intellect in a field or fields of which very few could have either the expertise or the interest.

Although it was now years since he'd begun to devise his revenge, it was only months since Adams had returned and he could now seriously start to plot a means to destroy this man who had ruined his life's work.

His mother had taught him the value of revenge; its exquisite joy, the way it could vivify your life, fire your every motive. He'd always known that his wastrel father had deserved to die in ignominy; although she never told him flatly that that was the case. It was the way she spoke about him obliquely, wheedled around the subject, made it overwhelmingly clear even if never outrightly stated, that his father was a worm, a parasite, a wife-beating shithole who deserved the poisonous death she'd administered.

And now the moment had come to exact that richly deserved revenge that awaited William Adams.

It was important that Adams should not face this without warning; his punishment must be refined and extended, particularly now that it could be exacted on top of the loss of his fucking black wife and their fucking stillborn child.

It was clear that the best way to exact revenge would be to give a clear warning: to extend his apprehension of what was about to happen; to draw out his suffering. But how best to do this?

He decided that a cryptic warning would be the best way to start the process, to increase the agony.

And now, having had weeks to think about it and after multiple recensions, he typed what was to be the first message:

MET= ES & HG

CL.E.VER. BUT …

Now, how best to deliver it?

CHAPTER 6

It was now late April and there was an early promise of summer. William walked along the awkward cobbles of Merton Street in his shirtsleeves, his tie loose and jacket slung over his shoulder. It was still light and there were few people about.

He cut left into Logic Lane, emerging in The High by the entrance to University College. William's host, his philosopher friend Andrew Strawson, stood at the front door, waiting to greet him. They'd known each other since school; their careers taking a roughly parallel path with Strawson now a Professorial Fellow at Univ.; his specialism was the now rather old-fashioned descriptive metaphysics.

Andrew had kept in contact with William during his Australian interlude and, on Gill's death, he'd written the most genuinely moving letter of condolence William had received. Their friendship was unforced and deep in that rather standoffish way the English cherished, without appearing to spend any effort in cultivating it.

They shook hands at the threshold.

'William, it's *so* good to see you,' said Andrew, shepherding him towards the Senior Common Room.

'And you, Andrew. It's been a long time … I must thank you for your lovely letter. I'm sorry I didn't reply … it's just …'

'Let's speak no more about it,' said Andrew, touching William briefly on the forearm.

William was reminded of how different were his relationships with his male friends in Australia. Here reserved, ordered, yet deep after years and without it being recognised; there, while initially shallow, growing to an affectionate and demonstrative depth over time.

'Look, William ... I'm afraid I have a confession.'

'Oh ... Yes?'

'It only occurred to me this evening ... I'd forgotten all about it. It's been a long time and so much as happened ...'

'What is it you're trying to say, Andrew?'

'Look ... Well. Robin's here. I mean, I should have known she'd be here. She is a Fellow, after all. But ... but, I just didn't think, I'm afraid.'

'Andrew, it's perfectly fine. I'm a big boy. I'm sure Robin will be at ease with me being here as I shall be with her.'

This was not strictly true. Dr Robin Atwell, Fellow in Roman Tort, lawyer, brilliant intellect, and stunning beauty, had been William's girlfriend for a brief time before his expedition to Babylon. Indeed, she had been part of the reason he'd gone: they'd had a disastrous seventh date during which she'd walked out on him, charging him with spinelessness, indecisiveness, and being unfeeling; at least that was his abiding memory of their last encounter.

The following day, he'd been invited to Babylon by Dom Taylor. William had tried to contact Robin to apologise before his departure but she'd not answered his calls.

And now, as they entered the SCR, here she was: begowned and talking animatedly in a small group on the far side of the room. In spite of the hundred or so people in the noise-filled space, he spotted her immediately.

Robin was tall, spare without being angular, and possessed of a grace which was as unusual as it was arresting. Her short, dark hair, upon which she spent little time, sat perfectly, as if recently coiffed by an expert. Her eyes were sky blue and her lips were, William remembered, generously kissable.

'What can I get you to drink?' asked Andrew.

'Eh ...?'

'A drink?'

'Oh, sorry. I was daydreaming.'

It wasn't true. He was thinking of that ill-fated night she'd walked out on him. And here she was, just as beautiful as ever, now looking in his direction. He registered her surprise, even shock, as he dipped his head while smiling at her.

Without a word, she left her small group and wended her way through the crowd, straight towards him.

'Drink?' Andrew persisted.

'G and T,' he muttered still intent on Robin's advance.

As Andrew departed, Robin reached William and threw her arms around him. She held him to her, a little too tightly and a little too long. He could feel her breasts pressing into him and felt the first sexual stirring he'd known since before Gill's death.

Still holding him to her, she whispered in his ear, 'I'm *so, so* sorry.'

Genuinely flustered, as he was discombobulated, he disengaged, still holding her by her arms, to look into her eyes.

'What have you to be sorry about?' he asked, genuinely puzzled yet warmed by the mostly happy memories of their earlier relationship.

Still looking at him intently, she said, 'I'm sorry that your wife and child died. I can't begin to imagine what you've been through. I'm sorry I didn't write to tell you that.

'I'm sorry I didn't return your calls before you left for Iraq.

'I'm sorry I made false accusations about you.'

'You did what?!' He was startled. What on earth could she be referring to?

'I accused you of being spineless. Of being unable to commit.'

'Oh ... that.' She was referring to the night she broke with him. 'Well ... I was ...'

'Your life, which I followed in prurient detail in the press, has proved beyond doubt that you're not spineless. And your marriage shows you can commit. Although it was simply not *me* you could commit to ...'

And with that, tears began to form in her eyes.

'Oh William. I am *so* sorry.'

He removed his pocket handkerchief and wiped away her tears.

'I've regretted, ever since that day, that I let you go,' she said.

At which point, Andrew returned with two G & Ts.

'Oh, hello Robin. I see you two are reacquainted.'

'Hello, Andrew. It's kind of you to get me a drink.' And with that she took the gin and tonic Andrew had intended for himself and downed a third of it in one go.

'Ah ... yes. I'll get myself one then,' he said, scurrying off to the bar again.

'I'm sorry about that. But I've said it,' she said, still looking ill-at-ease but somehow determined.

William felt confused. He was at once uneasy by all Robin had said: what did it mean? Why had she blurted it out like that? Yet, at the same time, he was relieved that she clearly had forgiven him his feckless behaviour of years before. He didn't know how to respond.

'Shall we sit together?' she said, taking him by the arm as the crowd made its way to the dining hall. William allowed himself to be led there, his mind a condign whirl of confusion.

The dining hall, formerly once the mediaeval great hall, was grand, sporting portraits of former Masters, and stained-glass windows celebrating famous alumni: Crick and Watson, of DNA fame, Percy Bysshe Shelley, Stephen Hawking.

The silver service *degustation* menu was accompanied by different wines with every course. It did not take long for the lubricated company to become jolly.

But William was still at a loss. Robin, in spite of many dates and liaisons in the interim since they had last seen each other, made it very clear that she regretted deeply letting William slip through her fingers. She had, back then, fallen in love with him – that was why she had reacted so angrily at his indecisiveness – and was in love with him still.

It was all rather too much for William to take in, not least of which because his mind was still racked by his loss of Gill.

Robin had talked of her life at length when she stopped abruptly. She put her hand on his and said, 'I'm sorry. I've been bloody insensitive, I know. It's just that all of this has been pent up for almost three years now ...'

'That's the sixth time you've said "sorry" since I arrived,' he smiled.

Her relief was palpable.

They talked throughout the evening and when it came time for the guests to leave she asked him if he would like to dine with her the next week.

She would have liked to say 'tomorrow' but realized she'd subjected him to a barrage of stored-up frustration and longing.

CHAPTER 7

The early summer sun shone gently through the gaps around his bedroom curtains. He woke groggily, taking time to orientate himself: first, time of day, then country, then the certainty that he was in his bed, in College. He put on his dressing gown and padded to the kitchen to make his first coffee of the day. He pondered recent events: his return to Oxford, his weekly trips to London, his renewed work at the Taylor Institute, Larry Verity, his life back in Claire's safe pair of hands, his Regius Professorship, and now his reunion with Robin. And all of this, each momentous in its own way, overshadowed by the hole in his heart created by Gill's death.

As he walked from the kitchen to the drawing room, past his front door, he noticed the paper sitting on the carpet; it had been posted through his letterbox. That, in itself, was odd: all mail was placed in pigeonholes by porters at the Lodge. This therefore must be an internal note, delivered by a resident in College.

Having collected it, he opened it as he sat in his chair by the fireplace to drink his coffee.

It was simply a single piece of unlined paper, folded in half. His puzzlement increased as he read the typed note:

MET = ES & HG

CL.E.VER. BUT …

What on earth did it mean? It was clearly cryptic. But what did the letters stand for?

'Met' was a common abbreviation for the Metropolitan Police, based at New Scotland Yard.

ES and HG could be people's initials but if that was the case then what did the "=" signify?

Alternatively, a word meaning Metropolitan Police might be an anagram of ES, HG, CL, and E.VER, possibly even including BUT. But the full stop and the three following dots suggested that 'but' really did mean but …

He plotted the possible anagram letters in a cloud:

CVLHEGESER

And his first thought was that there were too many letters for one word. Maybe it was two? More? Obviously, it could be 'clever' as it was written, minus the full stops. But what then to make of ES/HG? He could think of no such word. Maybe the ampersand represented an A. So: AESHG? But he couldn't make an anagram out of that either.

But then it occurred to him: who, in College, would post such a puzzle through his door, and why? He had no idea. Maybe the answer lay in the puzzle itself?

Could it be that this was not an anagram but, as at first he thought, personal initials? Apart from Metropolitan Police, he could think of no one with the initials MET. What of ES? Likewise, he drew a blank. Then what of HG? Well, that could be Hamish Grant, both a Fellow and a man who saw himself as a rival to be the next Provost.

But what then of CL? There was a boy at school called Colin Levenson. But that seemed unlikely. Just as unlikely that E.VER was someone's initials, as opposed to the word 'ever'.

William finished his coffee and was about to crumple the note and throw it in the bin when something at the back of his brain told him to keep it.

Having spent much of his life deciphering uncracked languages, this, surely, should be relatively simple. He would puzzle over it at his leisure.

He would forgo breakfast today and make his way straight to the Institute to take up his work on the letter *Nûn*.

But try as he may, he could not escape the riddle of the note and who in College might have posted it.

CHAPTER 8

They'd agreed on The Ivy: it was almost equidistant between their colleges and both liked it, William in particular because the cocktails were always first-class.

William had arrived early and was seated at the bar as Robin was shown through the front door by the waitress. As always, she looked stunning. She wore a short black cocktail dress, a sexy lawyer's dress, he thought. Although seldom did lawyers look so drop-dead gorgeous.

The restaurant, as usual, was packed. The ambient hubbub mercifully not exacerbated by the seemingly ubiquitous muzak that irked him so.

The walls in brightly embossed wallpaper of vibrant tropical scenes were barely visible behind the large and exotic framed prints which covered almost every inch. The place exuded a glamour of yesteryear.

William rose from the bar to greet her. He was nervous in that Robin had made her intentions clear at the dinner at Univ, and he felt by no means ready to find a place in his heart for the hole left there by Gill's death.

At Univ, Robin had been full-on, unrestrained. He'd agreed to this date because he felt he had no other option but he decided he would make it clear to her that he was not yet ready to start again.

He was a little surprised that she returned his demure peck on the cheek in like fashion before they settled into their table on the far wall benches.

Clearly, Robin was ill-at-ease.

'Robin, what's wrong?'

She looked away, as if embarrassed. 'I've been thinking about my behaviour at last week's dinner. To be honest: I've not been thinking about much else …'

He knew now what troubled her.

'Robin, please … Don't …'

'No. Let me say it.'

He was silent.

'I behaved with the sensitivity of a teaspoon. I didn't know you'd be there. I didn't have a chance to plan how I would act.

'I knew we'd bump into each other at some point now that you were back in Oxford, but I just … Well, I just wasn't ready …'

'Robin …'

'No. Let me finish …'

William sat back in his chair, resigned to have to allow Robin to torture herself thus.

'… I can't unsay what I said last week and in some respects I don't want to. I meant what I said: I've loved you ever since we dated and I love you still …

'But I know that my love is not reciprocated. And I know that what I said must've been hugely embarrassing for you, and I know that my behaviour, on top of your grief, must've been intolerable.

'I can't begin to tell you how sorry I am. I'm not really like that … insensitive, I mean. It's just that I'm 32, I don't want to put up with the cant and hypocrisy, or with the lies I've been telling myself since you left my life.

SAME PLAY, DIFFERENT ACTORS

'So I've decided to make a clean breast of it: I know I was wrong to confront you as I did. I apologise. I know you don't love me. So I've decided I would say my piece and leave you to grieve in peace … as I should have done last week.'

She was now crying freely.

William didn't know why he said: 'Why are you so sure I don't love you?' But he said it in the confidence that it did not sully Gill's memory to ask.

Robin, clearly, was stunned. She sat mute. William felt the need to fill the gaps.

'I sometimes feel that my life is utterly worthless without Gill. I think of her all the time and the pain is unbearable.

'But I'm not the man …'

The waitress, smiling, with impeccable timing, interrupted: 'Can I take your drink orders?'

William sighed. Robin dabbed at her eyes. The waitress, too late, realised she'd bungled.

'Oh … sorry … shall I come back later?'

'No. It's fine,' said William, regretting that their discussion had been conducted in public. 'I'll have an extremely dry vodka martini. Shaken, not stirred. Straight up. Preferably Polish vodka. But not Zubrowka. And Robin, what would you like?'

'I'll have a Bellini, please.'

In a way, the interruption was welcome. The gravity of both their confessions might have been too overwhelming.

As the waitress left, William said, 'Now, where was I?'

'You were about to tell me, I think, that you're not the man I once dated …'

'I was. And I'm not. If I'd had the opportunity …' He might well have said: *if you'd given me the chance …*

'I would have begged your forgiveness and asked for another

chance. And in a way, that's what I'm saying now, except … Gill is there… all the time. And I don't yet see how I can change my life to live with anything but a broken heart …'

Robin was now, gently, crying again.

William was also near to tears. He'd hoped he'd not been disloyal to Gill but he hoped, equally, that he'd not misled Robin: maybe there was hope for them? Maybe his grief would melt into sorrow which somehow would permit at least a glimmer of love? He didn't know.

The drinks arrived, the waitress now timid in taking their orders.

Over the food, as much to lighten the miasma of guilt that surrounded them both as anything else, William showed Robin the note he'd received that morning. As a lawyer, maybe she'd be able to make something of it.

'What do you make of this?'

'When did you get it?'

'It was slipped through my door last night.'

'Not in your pigeonhole with the porters?'

'No.'

'So, from someone in College?'

'It would appear so.' Clearly, they both came to the same conclusion. She studied the note at length.

'Do you think this is some kind of joke?'

'I really don't know. I tried to decipher it but pretty much came up blank.' He explained what he'd made of the initials, of possible anagrams. But none of it made sense.

Robin sat still, the note in her hand, clearly cogitating. 'What if MET is not Metropolitan Police but simply the word "met"?'

'But then "met" with an equals sign makes no sense.'

'The whole thing is in upper case, so MET could easily be "met". And what if it's not an equals sign?'

'Then what could it be?'

'Suppose your author is not computer savvy. Suppose they wanted to write the usual abbreviation for "with"…'

She drew the symbol 'with' on a paper napkin. 'Suppose they didn't know you could type "with" by pressing Alt plus whatever it is. So they did an = as its closest approximation?'

William was not clear what she was getting at.

'Suppose it doesn't mean "MET equals" but "met with" … That would mean that whoever wrote this met with ES, whoever he or she is, and HG, presumably Hamish Grant …?'

'So if you're right: what about the rest of it?'

'Well, the result of the meeting might have been …' she wrote it out 'clever, or it might have been some sort of lever, qualified by whatever C stands for.'

'I suppose it's possible. But it all seems rather convoluted.'

'I agree. But surely the hint of an answer lies in the three dots … at the end. There is more to come. You're going to get another note.'

By now, both of them had, in this linguistic diversion, overcome the earlier awkwardness of their shared confessions.

They finished the meal happily, intrigued by the cryptic message which they decided might, after all, be nothing more than a teasing joke.

William, however, could not escape the conviction that it was something more portentous.

CHAPTER 9

William's tutorial with Larry left him feeling even more uneasy than he had at their last meeting. After months of prevarication and excuses of 'illness', Larry had, as William suggested, prepared a brief paper on rebus in the Gilgamesh Epic.

As they sat, awkwardly, in William's drawing-room, William perused Larry's offering:

After the rise to power of the city of Babylon in the 18th century, under its most famous ruler, King Hammurapi (1792 – 1750 BC), the land of Sumer and Akkad was ruled by Babylon. Though the people of Sumer and Akkad did not themselves refer to their homeland as Babylonia, which is a Greek term, it is customary to call them Babylonians from this time onwards. Sumerian had by then died out among the people as a spoken language, but it was still much in use as a written language. Mesopotamian culture was nothing if not conservative and since Sumerian had been the language of the first writing, more than 1000 years before, it remained the principal language of writing in the early second millennium. Much more was written in the Babylonian dialect of Akkadian, but Sumerian retained a particular prestige…

This was only the first paragraph of his paper but, even still, it rang a bell: William had read this, or something very much like this, before.

He rose, went to his bookshelves behind the sofa on which they sat, and retrieved a copy of *The Epic of Gilgamesh* translated by Andrew George. George, he vaguely remembered, had run a pub in Surrey before becoming Professor of Babylonian at the University of London's School of Oriental and African Studies.

And sure enough, on thumbing through the introduction, he found on page xviii exactly the words he'd just read. Larry hadn't even bothered to try to mask his plagiarism; he'd simply typed out exactly what George had written in his introduction to the Penguin Classics edition of *The Epic*.

'Larry, you've simply copied bits out of this book and presented it to me as if it were your own writing. Surely you know this is plagiarism? What's going on here?' William was alarmed.

'I'm just finding my feet. You asked me to look at *The Epic*. I know nothing of Babylonia or cuneiform, or that kind of stuff. And since you put me under such pressure to get this done, I just copied it out.

'I know I could have done better, but I'm still settling in. You know: getting used to a new way of living and all. It was the best I could do given the time.'

'Larry, you've had a couple of months to get this done. You didn't think to tell me that you needed more time or support?'

'I didn't want to mess things about.'

'Well, you've certainly managed to do that.'

'Yeah, I'm sorry. Just give me a bit of time to settle in … you know … get my bearings …'

William felt deeply uneasy. He'd rarely encountered such bald-faced plagiarism. All essays presented to tutors could be put through a university program with algorithms that could identify any more than four words strung together in the same order as anything previously published. But Larry's offering was so obvious that William hadn't even needed to go to that trouble: here was a first class piece of intellectual theft practised by a student with a top degree from an Ivy League university in the States. What on earth was going on here?

He'd felt wary of taking on such a commitment but never had he dreamed that his fears would be realized so immediately. Already he was regretting giving in to Andy's blandishments.

'Larry, I don't really know about Princeton, or the United States more generally. But at Oxford – and I know this is rare, if not unique – a doctorate has to be an original contribution to knowledge. I'm quoting our constitution here: *'an original contribution to knowledge'*. What you've done, in trying to pass off someone else's words as your own, is hardly that. It's plagiarism and it's enough, in itself, for me to withdraw as your supervisor.

'But because these are difficult circumstances, and because I'm returning a favour for your uncle, I'm willing to overlook this … this mistake. But I won't countenance such a thing again. I expect your own work, original work from now on.

'I suggest that you go back to square one: have a look at the Rebus Principle in early Babylonian literature and come back to me, in two weeks' time, with your own thoughts on the matter.'

The meeting did not end well. Larry clearly resented not only the exposure of his plagiarism but also William's demands about how his failings might be rectified.

CHAPTER 10

William did get another note, two nights later, and it was portentous. It said:
... YOU'RE GOING TO DIE

Together, both notes then read:

MET = ES & HG

CL.E.VER. BUT ...

YOU'RE GOING TO DIE

He phoned Robin who picked up first ring.

'You've got to call the police,' said Robin after he told her what the note contained.

There was too much *déjà vu* here for William: he'd received a similar note, posted through the front door of his Mayfair home, while he and Ellie enjoyed an interlude between stints in Babylon. In fact, that earlier death threat had led to the team's return to the excavation site in Iraq.

And now it was happening again. The insecurity of those days when his and Ellie's lives were threatened by ISIS came flooding back.

'Would you mind talking to the police with me?' he asked. 'Maybe your theory about what it means might lead to something?'

'Of course. I'll be there in 10 minutes.'

Robin doubted there was any great value in her earlier speculation about what the note might have meant but she jumped at the opportunity to spend more time with William and possibly to be of help.

It was nearly three hours later that the police arrived at William's rooms in Oriel and it was made clear to him that they'd come so promptly precisely because of their memory of the earlier threat.

William was sufficiently distracted not to recognise DS Barcley, now Inspector Barcley, the man who had assisted in an earlier investigation when William's doctoral student had been murdered by a rogue faction operating within the Roman Catholic Church.

But once he remembered the policeman, he was overwhelmed by yet more *déjà vu*.

'Would you like a gin, Inspector?' asked William making his way to the drinks cabinet.

'Yes. I would. Thank you.'

'Let me do it, William,' said Robin.

As she prepared the drinks, William showed the detective the two notes.

'How did you get these?'

'They were both slipped through my door at night, the first, three days ago, the second, last night.'

'We assume they came from someone within the College,' said Robin from the drinks cabinet. 'Strangers can't really get past the Porters' Lodge and all incoming mail is via pigeonholes there.'

'So you think these were posted internally and at night?' asked Barcley.

'Yes.'

And then they went through their various theories of what the notes might mean: anagrams, personal initials, the Metropolitan Police, and so on.

They were disabused of the proposition that the notes were posted internally when Barcley's sergeant arrived to tell them that the porters had confirmed that three nights ago, and again last night, a small pane of glass by the door handle to the guestrooms on the King Edward Street site had been smashed. The dates corresponded with the delivery of William's notes.

'I don't believe in coincidences,' said Barcley.

Although the policeman did not understand the significance of the broken glass, William and Robin clearly did.

'What?' said Barcley.

William explained: 'The block of buildings adjacent to the College is called the King Edward Street site; it is owned by the College. It houses administration, some accommodation for Fellows, some storage, that sort of thing.

'It also has two suites of guestrooms. These are mostly empty but they are used occasionally for the visiting guests of College personnel. Every college,' he explained, 'has them.'

Not everyone understood the idiosyncrasies of the college system: there was no object, *per se*, corresponding to the proper noun 'Oxford University'; that entity was nothing more than a federation of colleges, 43 of them, each reduplicating the same function and product as the others, in varying degree. The colleges differed in shape and size and age but it was wealth that was the single most distinguishing factor. St John's, worth billions, was the richest, and some of the smaller halls scraped by each year sighing in relief if bankruptcy had been yet again averted. The wealth of some was prodigious: it was said one could walk from Oxford to Cambridge, a distance of 103 miles, without stepping off land owned by Brasenose College.

'Although they can be accessed internally, there are also external doors to both sets of guestrooms from King Edward Street.

'If someone has broken into the guestrooms, they can easily access the internal corridor outside the rooms and from there they can access the tunnel to the College ...'

'What?!'

Barcley thanked Robin who handed him and William double gins. William hefted a calming draft.

'Sorry ... I'm not being clear. For ease of access and to integrate the college with the King Edward Street site, there is a tunnel linking the site with the last quad of the College. If someone breaks into a guestroom, they simply have to go into the internal corridor, down a flight of stairs, and through the tunnel into the third quad, and from there, there is no obstacle to get into this quad where we are now and post a note through my door.

'I suspect, Inspector, contrary to what Robin and I had thought, that the note-writer is from outside the College.'

'Well, that extends the range of suspects,' said Barcley, clearly frustrated.

'The only way we can narrow that range is if we can decipher that first note,' Robin offered.

'Unless, of course, it's someone from within the College trying to make it appear as if it's someone from without ...' William swallowed the comment as too ridiculous.

'But why would anyone go to so much trouble? Particularly given it might be nothing more than a sick joke?' Robin offered.

Barcley, out of his depth, sat sipping his gin.

'I'll keep these notes, if I can...'

William mentally corrected 'can' to 'may'.

'... and get our experts to have a look at them.' By 'experts' he meant someone from the forensic team who was cleverer than he. Alternatively, he might send them to the Met for analysis.

'Yes, of course,' said William. 'But what should we do in the meantime? I mean … if there is really someone out there who wants to kill me?'

Barcley and his sidekick left, proffering bland assurances that this was probably nothing more than a prankster: most of these threats come to nothing.

Of course, neither Robin nor William believed him.

During the rest of the afternoon, they sat pondering the copies of the notes William had made, and William told Robin more of the threat he and Ellie had received from ISIS in London and of subsequent events.

She already knew much of the story from the newspapers of the time which she'd read avidly. It was interesting how different and revealing it was to hear the tale from William's perspective, especially when it entailed Ellie's involvement: he clearly had been in love with her.

Robin wanted to know what had become of Ellie but thought it better not to ask. They decided to take the ten-minute stroll up St Giles to Brown's for dinner: a well-made cocktail would doubtless revive their spirits, William thought.

CHAPTER 11

The next paper William received from Larry, via the Porters, was even more odd than the last.

As far as William could discern, it did not entail any plagiarism. But then, he would not be in a position to know because the essay was written on a field that had nothing whatsoever to do with Egyptology, Babylon, or the Rebus Principle.

For reasons that lay beyond William's imagination, Larry had written a piece on The Grand Inquisitor from Dostoyevsky's *The Brothers Karamazov*: a discussion between Ivan and Alyosha, two of the brothers Karamazov, about a tale set in sixteenth century Seville in Spain where a cardinal, the Inquisition's Grand Inquisitor, appears to interview a prisoner, who clearly, and anachronistically, is Christ.

The essay was rambling, florid in places, and utterly incomprehensible. Conclusions, preceded by 'therefore' and lacking premises, were drawn. Statements bearing no relation to anything arising from Dostoyevsky, as far as William could recall from his reading of the book twenty years before, were offered categorically. The whole thing was bizarre.

William was at a loss as to what he was being presented with, what possible relevance it might have for a doctoral offering and, indeed, about the sanity of its author.

William decided that he needed to speak with Larry as a matter of urgency; he was beginning to worry that he was unwell. But requests, via Larry's pigeonhole in the Porters' Lodge, for a meeting within that week went unanswered.

Early the next week, another essay arrived. As far as William could discern, it was a summary of Aristotle's *Poetics*:

Poetry is the imitation of human life in its universal aspects. The arts differ according to the medium, manner, and objects of imitation. Tragedy is the imitation of serious action, achieving through pity and fear a catharsis of those emotions ...

And while what was written seemed to be not unrepresentative of what Aristotle might have written, it had no relevance whatsoever to a doctoral thesis in Meroitic. More worryingly, various words had been scored heavily, underlined in red pen: *tragedy, tragic hero, character flaws, denouement.* Again, William was at a loss.

But while he could make nothing of this third, odd essay, he knew he could not let this go on any longer. He began to suspect that Larry was seriously unwell.

His first action was to advise the Provost, via a terse note covering the facts, of what had transpired. Then he contacted the College's Student Counsellor and finally, he rang the Chaplain who, it transpired, had been seeing Larry for 'spiritual support' on a regular basis. And while Father Penrose was happy to say that he had 'seen' Larry, professionally as it were, he was unwilling to divulge what had gone on in their 'confidential' sessions.

The following morning, William, promptly, at 9.00am, knocked on the door to Larry's apartment in the Woodstock Road clutching the three essays which had been the cause of his alarm. The door was opened almost immediately and there, looking just as *neat* as ever, was Larry.

'Ah, Professor. It's good to see you. Please come in,' he said, dripping *bonhomie*. William was taken aback: Larry was smartly turned out, he was charming, his rooms were neatly arranged and spotless. He seemed to be a different man from the surly, resentful fellow Willaim had last spoken with.

'Thank you, Larry. Look, I've come to talk to you about these,' and he brandished Larry's now crumpled papers in his hand.

'Oh, that. I fear there's been a misunderstanding.'

'A what ... misunderstanding?' William was flummoxed. 'I asked you to write a piece on Rebus in *Gilgamesh* and you present me with a peroration on Dostoyevsky! And then, quite out of the blue, I get a paper on Aristotle's *Poetics*! I confess I'm at a loss to know what's going on here.'

'Professor, please let me explain. Please have a seat,' he said, motioning to one of two leather-bound chairs sitting around a fireplace with an empty grate.

Once William was settled, Larry, having offered him coffee which William refused, resumed his charm offensive: 'I fear, Professor, there's been a serious misunderstanding. And it's entirely my fault.

'At Princeton, all teaching is via lectures. Here it's via tutorials. I gather that it's possible to do a degree without attending a single lecture ... astonishing! But I'm just trying to find my feet. At home, we could pursue pretty much anything that took our fancy, that was representative of the reading we were doing at the time, and that would be seen to be something that contributed to our general education ...'

'But ...' William was about to object. But before he could, Larry pressed on.

'I realize it's different here. It's my mistake. And I'm sorry. I think I now understand that doctorates here are very different from at home. And I realize that I have to be much more focussed on the dissertation topic than I might otherwise have expected.

'And I promise that that is exactly what I will do from now on ...'

William still felt, in spite of Larry's excuses, very uneasy. But before he could express that unease, Larry pressed on.

'In fact, since we last spoke, I've had an idea about how I might proceed. You said that you were mystified as to how, with so little actual script, Rebus might be extracted from what Meroitic is available. But I've had an idea ...'

'Yes ...?' said William doubtfully.

'Yes. Well ... Rebus is well-identified in classical Egyptian script ... so if I research all known Meroitic texts and look for any parallels with Egyptian then I might be able to establish a correlation between the two. If that is the case, then the Egyptian might provide an insight from its own Rebus development, a baseline as it were, into possible Meroitic examples of Rebus.'

William was shocked. The idea, on the face of it, had merit. If, for example, small samples of the writing, say, prepositional phrases, were duplicated between the two languages, then this might afford a chance to identify Rebus development of the Egyptian and, by comparison, a similar evolution in Meroitic.

In fact, it was such a good idea that, if pursued rigorously, it might just work!

William was lost for words.

'Well, what do you think, Professor?'

'It might well have merit,' said William before he had a chance to consider the linguistic implications of Larry's proposal.

'Great! I'll just get on with that if you're ok with it?'

William still, in the light of their earlier encounters, felt uneasy. But as he could see no reason why this avenue of research should not be followed and as Larry was now proving amenable, even apologetic, he felt he simply could not refuse. But he needed, much against his own natural inclination, to lay down the law: 'I need to give this more thought, Larry. But if your proposal does have merit, then, of course, I'd be happy for you to pursue it.

'But I must make myself perfectly clear: there are to be no further excursions into areas entirely unrelated to Rebus and Meroitic. There are to be papers presented every fortnight which represent the progress you've made since our previous meeting. There is to be full exposure of all sources used ...' both men understood that this was a reference to Larry's earlier plagiarism.

'Absolutely,' said Larry, beaming.

William left Larry's flat, happy that he'd managed to achieve what he set out to do; happy that Larry had accounted, albeit not entirely convincingly, for his strange behaviour; happy with the intriguing suggestion Larry had made to resolve the Rebus difficulties of identification that they'd discussed before. But unhappy, in spite of all these assurances: something was not quite right.

CHAPTER 12

The notes delivered, it was now time to execute revenge.

He sat in the study, at the same computer where he'd composed the notes. Accessing the dark web was a straightforward affair: he used the TOR network to open a surprisingly popular assassins' message board and typed in *aconite*. He would wait for a week or two to strike, but now was the time to prepare.

He relished the thought, about which he felt confident, that they would have involved the police and that neither of them would be able to decipher the simple puzzle he'd set them. He knew Adams was being helped by the Atwell woman. Oxford gossip afforded little privacy. True, he deliberately introduced two elements to confuse them – the letter transposition and redundant full-stops. And when they'd cracked the notes they would marvel at how stupid they had been.

But by then it would be too late anyway.

Aconite is one of the most efficacious poisons in the apothecary's armoury; it kills in seconds, whether injected or ingested: ten seconds of lucid stupefaction, then death. Enough time to know that the notes' promise was fulfilled but not enough time to be able to do anything about it.

It would then take the most expert and alert of forensic pathologists to be able to identify the cause of death. To all intents and purposes, it would simply appear that the heart had ceased to function. He paid the £500 for the smallest effective dose – a sachet of powder, two inches square – and smiled at the irony that for an extra £5.99 it could be delivered the next day. Death commodified, he thought.

The idea, he found, aroused him sexually ...

♦ ♦ ♦

It was common knowledge in Oxford that William Adams was unique amongst dons in having a half bottle of red wine everyday he ate lunch in College. Thereafter, he would retire to his rooms for his equally well-known 'afternoon kip' of half-an-hour or so. Such vignettes were widely known thanks to the prurient detail tabulating the life of so famous a person by the voyeuristic British press, even though Adams himself never sought publicity and always shunned the myriad requests for interviews, exposés and the like.

It was equally well-known that Adams spent most Wednesdays at his club in London, the Athenaeum, England's premier gentleman's club (although much to William's chagrin, they now admitted women). It was the club of kings and princes, of Darwin and Dickens, of Wilberforce and Wellington.

He knew, therefore, when he would strike: a weekday, barring Wednesdays, at a time when Adams would lunch in College. It thus could be any day of his choosing: not only did dons have to sign in for lunches the following week (and discovering who had signed in was a relatively straightforward affair) but it was even easier: he'd hacked Adams' diary, prepared by his secretary Claire. She unwittingly provided him with all the information he needed.

Tomorrow, Tuesday, and three weeks to the day after he'd delivered the first note, he would strike. By the time they discovered how he'd done it, it would be too late.

In the early hours of Monday night, as per the previous two occasions, he made his way on foot down the Woodstock Road, through St Giles, and past Carfax into The High. There were no cars about as he slipped into King Edward Street. Since his first two break-ins, they'd installed CCTV on the College wall opposite, fifteen feet away. They'd not thought to improve the quality of lighting by the guestroom doors and his black jeans and shirt, together with the black balaclava he'd donned on entering King Edward Street, meant that they would not be able to identify him in a million years. To make identification more difficult, he removed his glasses and put on contact lenses.

He slipped his folded handkerchief onto the small pane, just above the door handle, the putty around it still relatively fresh, and, as he'd done with ease twice before, jabbed his car key sharply into the corner of the pane. The thin glass broke, falling silently into the carpeted interior. He removed the remaining shards and let himself in.

He stole silently towards Front Quad, confident in the knowledge that no further obstacles would present themselves: all colleges, complacent behind the huge locked wooden entrance gates, did not bother with tight security. Doors to chapels, staircases and, crucially, dining halls were all unlocked.

And so it was that he stepped silently from the dining hall into the Oriel College kitchens to begin his search for the object he required.

◆ ◆ ◆

One of the many tales in the life of William Adams, as recounted by embedded – and intrepid – *Mail* reporter Sam Wilson during William's stint in Babylon and the interlude in his Mayfair home where he'd received a death threat that led to their return to Babylon, had alluded to William's habit to take wine with every lunch; something, it appeared, *Mail* readers found interesting.

Wilson had noted how William had his half-bottle of wine – always claret – from an inscribed decanter once belonging to his beloved father.

It was this ephemeral vignette that had planted the seed in his mind when he first planned to kill Adams. And it was this inscribed decanter that he now sought as he fossicked through the tableware in the kitchen store behind the dining hall of Oriel College, Oxford.

And there it was, at the far end of the shelf of dozens of decanters, all identical. But this one had a solid silver neck, beautifully sculpted, and inscribed with the name *ADAMS*.

He put on his surgical gloves.

He wasted no time in removing the sachet from his pocket and opening it carefully. He poured the contents into the decanter and measured ten drops of water into it from a nearby sink. He swilled the water and crystals together until the liquid was clear and, replacing the stopper, left it back where it was, knowing that when the liquid dried it would leave an invisible residue in the base, there to contaminate whatever was put in the decanter.

He left by the same route he'd entered, slipping into the anonymity of the cloud-filled night. The whole procedure took less than half-an-hour.

All he had to do now was wait.

CHAPTER 13

It was Tuesday and William had spent a good part of the morning at the Taylor Institute slowly ploughing his way through entries for his *Lexicon*. It was unexciting work, but William enjoyed the methodical research it entailed and the fact that there were so many assistants there willing to undertake any necessary donkey work in the hope of a mention in forwards or footnotes.

He was particularly glad of the help of Dr Jack Sutherland, the other Meroitic expert at the Institute. More an historian than a linguist, Jack had a compendious knowledge of Nubia and was only too happy to share his insights and intellectual acumen with William. That morning, as William continued to plough his way through the letter *Nûn*, Jack had suggested a cross-reference to an inscription in Karnak, not unlike the Meroitic phrase William was researching. Might they have a common source? They were of a similar period. Could the Egyptian *hapax legomenon*, the phrase occurring only once in the language, *iw Nwt tn srwd N pn ssp.s,* be evidence of an attempt to translate a borrowed Meroitic sentence?

Jack's insights, and slightly different way of approaching things, were a real fillip for William.

On occasion, he felt these encounters almost confirmed him in his decision to return home.

It was in a reverie, remembering the time his dearest friend,

Ross Farnsom, had with great difficulty advised William for his own good to return home, that his phone rang. It was Robin. It was 11:45 and he sat in his office, the blazing sun shining through the large window at his back, with the door open to let what little breeze there was through.

'How about lunch?' she asked.

'I was just packing up. About to go for College lunch …'

'I think you'd be better off with me.'

'I'm sure that's always true,' he joked, 'but is everything okay?'

'Yes, everything is fine. Except, there's something I need to tell you.'

'Okay. The Ivy, Brown's or Quod?'

'Quod, please. I'll see you there in 15 minutes.'

'I'll ring the College to cancel. I look forward to seeing you.'

And so it was that that day Robin Atwell saved William Adams' life.

CHAPTER 14

William Adams was such a celebrity that securing a table at late notice was always possible. They sat away from The High-side front windows and to the left of the bar. William ordered a Margarita without salt and Robin her usual Bellini.

It wasn't until after they'd ordered their food, and following light-hearted chitchat, that Robin became suddenly serious.

'William, I'm sorry. But I've just heard something disturbing. You know my friend Annie?'

'Yes. She's a classicist at Univ.'

'That's right. Well … she's just told me that she was a guest at Christ Church dinner last night. And …' She was clearly reluctant to share her information.

'Go on.'

'Well … she overheard Hamish Grant, who was also a guest, sprouting to all who would listen that he had it on very good authority that …'

'Yes?'

'That much of your work is based on plagiarism.'

William was silent. He was staggered. This was one of the worst charges that could be laid at the feet of any academic.

'But that's preposterous! It was *I* who cracked the language. I've always acknowledged all my sources and support. There are only two others who are serious in this field ...' William was lost for words.

'I know. I know,' said Robin, visibly upset on William's behalf. 'But why would he say such things? Everybody knows of your probity. Why would he be so ghastly?'

The bar was now filling and in the hubbub no-one had noticed the anguish the pair of them suffered at Robin's news.

It was obvious to William what was happening. But he couldn't credit the venality of a man who would stoop so low to achieve his goals.

'I know what he's doing,' said William leaning closer to Robin to be heard above the noise.

For reasons that neither of them later understood, Robin mistook his movement to be something else and turned her head to kiss him full on the lips.

She was mortified when she realised her mistake. William smiled and, doubtless with Dutch courage, polished off his Margarita in one go.

'I think that calls for another, don't you?' And almost before he could beckon the waiter, a smartly turned-out young woman with short, brilliantined hair and a long white apron was at his side.

'Can I get you something?' she said.

William smiled again as he suppressed the mental correction of *can* to *may*.

'Yes. I'd like another.' And then, looking at a deeply embarrassed Robin, 'Would you ... No. We should celebrate. May I convince you to share a bottle of champagne with me?'

Robin nodded sheepishly.

'Your best bottle of champagne, please.'

'Of course, Sir,' said the waitress, mystified at what was going on but amused by it, whatever it was.

'I've always wanted to say that.'

'What?'

' "Your best bottle, please". It sounds so pretentious …'

'I must say you seem quite jolly given the news I've just given you.'

'I am. I realized this morning, maybe for the first time, that my friend Ross Farnsom was right in encouraging me to leave Australia. And I've realized, when you kissed me …'

'It was a mistake. I'm sorry. I thought you were … I didn't mean to …' Robin blushed again.

'Oh, that's a pity. I quite enjoyed it.'

Robin was lost; she'd never seen him in this mood before. And especially given the news she'd just imparted.

'I was going to say that it's good we can make such mistakes with each other with such ease. And I was going to say that I knew why Grant is trying to besmirch my reputation.'

'It was only a tiny mistake,' she said, still overwhelmingly embarrassed at her blunder and holding up her index finger and thumb, narrowly spaced, to suggest a scintilla.

'What?! Besmirching my reputation was only a tiny mistake?' he smiled.

'No. Me kissing you, you fool.' And with that she placed her hand over his as he looked at her intently. Lovingly, she hoped.

When the waitress returned with a bottle of *La Grande Année Bollinger 1999*, they were still in light embrace, his lips brushing hers.

'I can come back later,' she said, clearly having no intention of doing so. 'You asked for the best bottle, and this is it. I'm afraid it's a magnum …'

'Oh, we'll get by somehow,' William smiled, Robin still holding his hand.

Over the meal, William explained how it was obvious that Grant was still jockeying for the post of Provost and was clearly trying to knock William out of the race.

'But I thought you told him you had no interest in it?'

'And so I did.'

'Well?'

'Clearly, he doesn't believe me.'

'What are you going to do?'

'I think I shall have to pay Professor Grant a visit.'

◆ ◆ ◆

It was now over a year since William had last made love. Since then, his life had been effectively celibate, although a number of women had made it clear they'd be happy to help him overcome his grief.

They'd spent the afternoon considering Grant's disgraceful behaviour and whether the notes meant that slander extended to threats of murder, with the HG standing for Hamish Grant.

An earthy bottle of Shiraz over dinner had followed the champagne and now they found themselves in each other's arms in William's bed. Although she'd never been happier, Robin wept gently onto William's chest. William, too, shed quiet tears of release, assured that Gill would want nothing but his happiness.

◆ ◆ ◆

The Porter's Lodge had called the kitchens to say that Professor

Adams would not, after all, be lunching in College.

By then it was too late.

The assistant to the sommelier had already decanted William's wine for the meal to let it breathe; it was a bottle of *Château Pavie, Saint-Émilion Grand Cru 2001*, chosen by Claire from his private collection held in the College cellars.

It was 11.50 am, approaching the time when the kitchen staff had their half-hour break to eat their own College-supplied meal before preparing for the onslaught of staff and students at 1.00 pm.

The assistant to the sommelier, the chef, and the sous chef, sat together for their lunch, as they always did.

'I've already decanted it,' said the assistant.

'It would be a pity to waste it. 2001 was quite a good year. It will be off by tomorrow. And, anyway, Professor Adams is always in London on Wednesdays.'

'I agree,' said the chef. 'Get three glasses would you, Charles?'

His under-chef collected three glasses and placed them in front of each of the steaming plates of *osso buco*. He sat.

The assistant poured the ruby liquid, the aroma assailing their nostrils over that of the veal. The combination, for people whose life's work was good food and drink, was heady. They raised their glasses.

'Cheers,' they smiled. A perfect accompaniment to a superbly cooked meal.

It was only the assistant sommelier who noticed a strange undertone to the wine as he finished his first mouthful.

Within ten seconds, the assistant sommelier, the chef, and the sous chef, were dead.

CHAPTER 15

Somehow, news of the death threat to William Adams became public and Sam Wilson, one-time author of the long-running and award-winning column of four years before, *The Babylonian Treasure Trove*, convinced his editor at *The Mail* that another column, centred on this most adventurous of archaeologists, was worth resurrecting.

Thus the threat to William's life was recounted – in sufficient detail to demonstrate a serious leak at Thames Valley Police headquarters – under Wilson's new daily column *Oxford Intrigues*.

Wilson had secured a photocopy of both death notes sent to Adams from his source at headquarters; they'd only cost him £1000.

His first column consisted of a brief introduction, followed by a reproduction of the notes.

He'd suggested to his editor that they should start a competition: a lifetime subscription to *The Mail* for anyone who was able to unravel the puzzle. The winner could be given 'The William Adams' Award for Decipherment'. A lovely irony.

The editor knocked the silly notion on the head.

Wilson went on to speculate about the meaning of the notes: the second was clearly a death threat but what could the first possibly mean?

Like William and Robin before him, he assumed that 'MET' meant Metropolitan Police. And as the Met contained the CTB, Britain's counterterrorism branch, he further assumed that, as had happened to William Adams before, this was a renewed threat from Islamic extremists.

If that were the case, what could ES and HG possibly mean?

He consulted *The Mail's* state-of-the-art maps.

While HG obviously meant Hamas-Gaza, what on earth was ES? East Syria? Certainly, ISIS operated out of East Syria. But then he encountered Deir ez-Zur, which, he knew, given the vagaries of transliteration, could, at a journalistic stretch, be ES, the Z becoming an S. But why Gaza and East Syria, or es Sur, for that matter? There was an el Sadad in the Homs District. ES? And an el Sukhnah in Palmyra. And then he discovered Hasbani Ghajar. So that might be HG? It was all becoming too confusing. And confusion did not sell newspapers.

He concluded his column by inviting any readers who had information on the subject to contact him. His in-tray was flooded with helpful suggestions, all of them useless.

CHAPTER 16

William woke the following morning to the sound of persistent banging on his door. He extricated himself from a still sleeping Robin, put on his dressing gown, and made his way groggily – doubtless the effect of yesterday's alcohol consumption – to the door.

'All right. I'm coming! No need for such a racket.'

He was greeted at the door by Detective Inspector Barcley. 'Good morning, Sir. May I come in?'

'Yes. I mean, no. What time is it?'

'It's eight o'clock, Sir.'

'What on earth can you be wanting at this hour?' said William, still waking.

'Three people in College are dead, Sir. I need to talk to you.'

'Who's that, William?' called Robin from the bedroom.

'And that would be … Dr Atwell?'

Too many questions. William was too shocked and hung-over to be particularly coherent.

'What? No … it's the police,' William called back to Robin over his shoulder. He heard scuffling and the door close.

'Who is dead?' said William, suddenly sober as the gravity of things fell upon him and sleep fell away.

'Look, Sir. This is not the place for such a discussion. Can I come in?'

It's *may* thought William, not *can*.

'Yes, of course. Sorry. Do forgive me. I'm afraid you woke me ... us. We had rather a late night.'

William ushered him into the hallway and closed the door behind him.

'I'd like to talk to you about that as well, Sir. Just where were you from lunchtime onwards yesterday? We've been looking for you everywhere!'

'Well, we were a hundred yards down the road from here. At Quod. We had lunch and dinner there. We got back here at about 10.00 or 10.30. But why? What's happened?'

By now, Robin had joined them. She was wearing the short, patterned dress from yesterday, looking crumpled, but as beautiful as ever.

Taking charge, she shepherded both men into the drawing room and sat them facing each other.

The early morning sun shone through the room's windows, shining off the polished, dark wooden panelling of the drawing room and throwing the pictures on the walls into sharp, colourful relief: a Laura Knight beach scene, a lesser painting by her husband John Lavery, and exquisite small landscape by Corot, and an even smaller scene of Argenteuil by Renoir.

'Do you have any tomato juice, William?' asked Robin.

'Yes. In the cupboard next to the fridge. Why?'

'I think we need a pick-me-up.'

'Oh.'

William sat in stunned silence until Robin returned with two Bloody Marys. He wanted her to be there for Barcley's news.

'Do you want coffee, Inspector?'

'No thanks.'

Once she'd settled, he told them how, the previous lunchtime, three of the kitchen staff had died – virtually simultaneously by all accounts – while eating their lunches.

Forensics had yet to confirm but the police were working on the assumption that it was poisoning.

'You mean deliberate?'

'Yes.'

'But that's so awful! Who would want to do such a thing?' asked Robin.

There was an ominous silence before Barcley said: 'We suspect that they were poisoned by the wine they shared. They were the only kitchen staff present who drank the wine. And the decanter is now with forensics. We should have answers today.'

'But what's that got to do with us?' asked Robin.

'They were drinking from *your* decanter,' said Barcley solemnly, looking at William.

'Oh,' said William.

It began to dawn: the anonymous notes, the wine poisoned; he was supposed to be there but cancelled at the last moment. Were he there, he would have drunk wine from his father's decanter.

The deaths were intended for him.

CHAPTER 17

William explained the nature of their conversation the day before: the slanderous comments of Professor Grant; William's perceived interest in the Provostship; William and Grant's earlier discussion about the post; and HG as part of the first note's riddle.

'But surely no one could stoop to murder over a simple job!?' complained William. He simply couldn't believe such a thing, not even of a bastard such as Grant.

'You'd be surprised at what counts as motive for murder, Sir.'

'But …'

'Don't you worry about it, Sir. We'll follow up on Professor Grant. We should be in a far better position later today when we have the results from forensics.'

'But what are we meant to do in the meantime?' asked Robin, draining the last of her Bloody Mary. 'And what if it's not him? Surely William's in danger until you've caught whoever has done this!?'

Barcley couldn't deny her conclusion but sought, ineffectually, to allay their fears.

William had been subject to such threats before and knew only too well that the police could do little to safeguard them against a determined attacker.

CHAPTER 18

It had been three weeks and William had heard nothing from Larry Verity: no essay on Rebus, no excuses or explanation for the no-show, no communication at all.

William already regretted having taken him on, but now he realized that this was not to be the usual workload normally generated by supervising a doctoral student. Larry was going to be extraordinarily difficult to guide through the demanding process of researching and writing up a 150,000-word *original contribution to knowledge*. And thus far, after two months, William had not received a single written word on the proposed topic of his thesis.

Broadly speaking, there were two ways to make an original contribution to knowledge: first, and most commonly, one simply found an area not covered before; something obscure or highly specialized. This was the easy option. Here little imagination was required and rarely was a thesis actually argued. An example of this was *The Theology of Laplace 1822-1823* which William had, years before, encountered and which had made him giggle: Laplace was a physicist and mathematician; his theology in those two years must have been momentous! Alternatively, it was a very short doctoral thesis.

The second, vastly more difficult, way was to present a thesis which shed new light on the world within one's discipline, presenting something that had never been argued before.

Here the argument might be proved wrong, the thesis itself misguided and the risk of failure was therefore amplified.

Larry's proposed thesis straddled both possibilities: if he could identify Rebus development in Meroitic then that would significantly contribute to the discipline's understanding of the Nubian tongue.

But Larry's work, inevitably, would depend on William's own research for his *Lexicon*. And he was only, with the letter *Nûn*, half-way through the alphabet. Larry's proposal was therefore parasitic on William's work, adding yet more pressure on him to complete the *Lexicon*. But supervising Larry's studies was a distraction from William's own research thereby impeding his own completion of the very work Larry would need to rely on: a classic catch-22!

All of this was exercising William as he sat at his desk with that morning's mail from the porters, contemplating the best way he might deal with the absence of work due from Larry.

It was thus, absent-mindedly, that he had an epiphany.

He'd just put the letter-opener down from a letter marked *From the Office of the Vice Chancellor*. Inside was a standard form: *Review of Doctoral Research*. And typed below the heading was Larry's name:

CLARENCE EVAN VERITY

At first, William thought nothing of it: his review would be brief. There was nothing to report. No relevant work had been submitted and the first essay due was still outstanding.

But then, without quite realizing how, it struck him: Larry's name. The first time he'd seen it in full. He'd not even realized that Larry was, in fact, Clarence.

Clarence Evan Verity, which could easily be shortened, using the initial letters, to: CL. E. VER. Condensed, it gave CL.E.VER., from the final line of the first note of the death threats.

Surely this couldn't be a coincidence? And if it wasn't then what did it mean?

MET= ES & HG

CL.E.VER. BUT ...

Was this a signature, crudely disguised? The murderer identifying himself? But why would he do that? And why would Larry want to kill William? What on earth could his motive possibly be?

But maybe it wasn't a signature? What if it was a reference to Larry by a third party, somehow implicating him? But that made no sense. Larry had not long arrived and would know only a few people in Oxford. Unless he was the note's author, why would anyone else, barely more than a fresh acquaintance, want to suggest that he could be guilty of murder?

More particularly, why would Dom's nephew want to kill him? It was precisely because of his happy relationship with Dom and his own expertise in the field that Larry had sought to be his student. To kill him would be like killing the goose that laid the golden egg! It all made no sense.

William phoned Robin.

CHAPTER 19

Much troubled, and while waiting for Robin to arrive, he continued with the rest of his mail. The letter had a large garish stamp of snakes and lizards. It was postmarked Sydney and gave Dr Ross Farnsom's name and address on the back.

The Mail's 'Oxford Intrigues' had been syndicated to *The Australian* and thus Ross had learned of William's predicament from his broadsheet newspaper.

He had also learned, from the fourth and fifth columns in the series, of William's 'liaison' with the 'Oxford beauty' and 'stellar intellect' Dr Robin Atwell, a woman he had dated previously. William, if the prurient press were to be believed, had finally found consolation in Dr Atwell's perfectly-formed arms after torturing himself over Gill's death. Ross had smiled, hoping that it was true. His friend deserved some happiness after all he'd been through. And Gill, he knew, would want William's happiness more than anything else.

But now, it appeared, he was thrust back into the hurly-burly of terrorist threats and international intrigue. He began to wonder whether he was right to have encouraged William to return to England.

William was sitting at his drawing room window, gin and tonic in hand, looking out over the perfectly manicured Front Quad, musing over exactly the same question, mentally trying to will the constriction of his breathing to abate, when his phone rang.

'G'day mate,' said Ross.

'Oh, Ross, hello. I was just thinking of you ... What time is it there?'

'Ten in the morning. Look, how are you my friend? I've been worried about you. The press over here are running amok with your adventures ...'

Is not *are*, thought William. *Press: it's a collective noun, so singular.*

'You know as well as anyone, Ross, that press reports are not to be believed. There's nothing for you to worry about ...'

'No death threats?'

'Well ... there has been one of those ...'

'No one dead? With you apparently the target?'

'Well ... it would appear so.'

'No *fatwa* announced by ISIS?'

'No. I haven't heard that one! Though it wouldn't surprise me ... I've been on ISIS hit-lists before ...'

'No threat to your new girlfriend, Robin?'

'Ah. I was meaning to tell you about Robin.'

'Mate, it doesn't sound like everything is hunky-dory over there. You're not tempted to come back?'

There was a pause.

'Ross, I'd be lying if I said I wasn't worried. And it's true that, until recently, I was asking myself if I'd made the right decision.

'But look ... since Robin and I have got together ...' He didn't know how best to finish the sentence, besides, it was as if it was only yesterday that they'd resumed their relationship. The threat still hanging over their heads meant that they both felt insecure and uncertain and yet their commitment to each other was growing stronger daily.

'I know it sounds crazy. Especially since I was the guy who suggested you went home in the first place. But I've been talking to Anthony ...' Anthony Elkin was Professor of Archaeology at the University of Sydney and William's former, nominal Head of Department and second-best man at his marriage to Gill, '... and he says that your old job is there any time you want it.

'You could come over, even if it's just for a break, and bring Robin with you. We'd all love to meet her. And, if you like, you could stay with Anne and I.'

It's accusative: it's not *I*, it's *me*, thought William.

Immediately, he chided himself. He had to stop doing it: mentally correcting other people's solecisms. It was not that he was being churlish or smart-arsed; it was rather that it, somehow, just came automatically, almost viscerally. And he had to stop it.

'Ross, that's so kind. And I'm sure Robin would love to meet you all too. But I don't think we can leave until this thing,' unconsciously, he left the 'thing' decidedly vague, 'is resolved.'

'I understand, mate. But don't forget us over here, or we'll just have to come and visit you there.'

'That would be a delight. Maybe once this has all blown over ...?'

They rang off, leaving William both assured of the depth of his friendship with Ross but in a quandary about what he and Robin should do while their lives remained under threat.

CHAPTER 20

Sam Wilson's breathless encomiums and idle speculation had ignited the Internet, again, not only of the readers of The Mail but of other newspapers, journals and TV, but also of the many would-be jihadists who had not forgotten William's earlier challenges to the purity of Islam.

He had dared, through the discovery and interpretation of pagan objects, to bring into question the historical truth behind the Faith as recorded by the blessed Prophet – peace be upon him.

And so it was that William's mailbag, apart from personal letters directed to the College or internal mail, sent to his post office box under Claire's oversight, burgeoned.

The number of death threats more than doubled each week, and therefore grew exponentially.

Claire, carefully and with gloved hands, perused William's mail and sent, by daily carrier, anything suspicious to Thames Valley Police, FAO DI Barcley. There, a small team assessed each piece, fingerprinted those deemed appropriate, and started investigations of those more promising.

Claire was almost overburdened with the increased workload but was energised by her small part in trying to keep William safe. Although she cursed, and contemplated sending anonymous death threats, to Sam Wilson.

A number of suspects were interviewed. Some were cautioned,

and two *Persons of Interest* were arrested and charged with making threats to life. Court cases would follow.

◆ ◆ ◆

The effect of local, national and now international speculation on William and Robin's fate (their future was now conjoined since Wilson revealed their 'liaison': they were seen 'holding hands' at a restaurant; they were observed 'gazing into each other's eyes'; it was believed that she 'often spent the night in his rooms in Oriel ('strictly against College rules')', and so on, was increasingly alarming for the both of them.

After William and Ellie's earlier experience during their brief time away from the dig in Babylon of being followed by reporters from *The Mail*, they began to worry whether they were now being tailed. Were their phones safe? Had friends been approached with offers of rewards for information?

Although they both knew that dwelling too intently on these matters was not a large step removed from paranoia, they couldn't help but feel oppressed, exposed, and vulnerable.

It was Claire who suggested to William that he and Robin might like to consider a getaway 'until all this shit blows over.' She mentioned Dorsoduro, the *sestiere* in Venice where William's apartment was.

Having met at his rooms following his revelation of Larry's apparent signature on the first death threat note, they adjourned to the restaurant for dinner. And so it was that in a banquette at the back of Brown's, they began to hatch a plan.

'It's just a small, two bedroomed flat in Dorsoduro, just behind Ca' Rezzonico on the Grand Canal …'

'But how could we get away?'

'I'm sure that given everything that's going on, you wouldn't have any trouble getting compassionate leave?'

'Probably.'

'I can pretty much do as I like with my commitments being so meagre.

'In the past, I've often used a private jet for travel. The flight plan can be kept secret. No-one would know where we're going. And Nonna keeps the place in good order. And she would kill anyone she thought threatened us. She is quite protective of me ... and quite ferocious.'

'Nonna?'

'Yes. Nonna Claudia. She is more than a housekeeper. She kind of adopted me when I was a boy when I used to go there with my father, after my mother died. I've gone there pretty regularly since my father died. And Nonna always spoils me rotten.'

Robin didn't need much convincing: as a lecturer in Roman tort, her Latin was first class and, as a consequence, her Italian was more than passable. She'd spent many holidays in Italy, particularly in Puglia, in the south. William, being a linguist, and having spent so much time there, was fluent.

And so it was decided: they would leave for Venice as soon as possible. They would tell no-one of their destination.

'Should we not tell the police?' asked Robin.

'Especially not the police,' said William. 'After all, we know that it must have been they who leaked our story to *The Mail* in the first place.'

'But what do we do about Larry? Or Mr CL.E.VER?' asked Robin.

'I just can't bring myself to think it's him. He's weird, and he's rude but ...'

'Sounds like the beginnings of a formula for a murderer to me.'

'I'd like some time to think about it. Anyway, there's no way he could know where we are so we'll be safe in Venice.'

'What about his supervision?'

'I'll come to some sort of arrangement with Claire. She'll be able to get his stuff to me. Anyway, I don't suppose we'll be there too long...'

They would leave in two days' time. Claire had arranged it all: in the dead of night, Rick, William's driver, would collect them from the College. At that time, it would prove relatively easy to ensure they had no tail. He would take them to Kidlington, to Oxford airport, where their hired jet would depart for Marco Polo arriving two and a half hours later. From there, Giorgio would pick them up in William's speedboat and drop them at the Ca' Rezzonico stop, a short walk away from his apartment, where Nonna would be waiting to greet them and, knowing her, overfeed them a generous breakfast.

Nonna had been told they might stay as long as a month.

Claire had prepared their excursion as meticulously and as privately as possible. She was confident they would not be followed. She wished it was she, not Robin, who was going to Venice with William but she knew that such fantasies of an older woman were better not dwelled upon.

CHAPTER 21

DI Barcley was at a loss over the disappearance of Professor William Adams and Dr Robin Atwell.

He had rung to arrange a meeting for an update. There was no answer. It seemed to William and Robin that Barcley's updates were a substitute for the fact that the police were singularly unable to guarantee their security.

After several attempts to contact them, Barcley decided to pay William a visit. He became increasingly concerned that there was no answer at his door; that the porters had seen neither of them for two days; and that a similar picture emerged from University College when he enquired of Robin.

A porter had shown him into William's rooms where it appeared, given the apparent absence of toiletries and underwear, he had left.

It was with foreboding, and with memories of an earlier disappearance when William and Laura Tennant had left for the south coast following the death of Laura's boyfriend, that Barcley decided that matters had taken a turn for the worse.

An All-Points Bulletin was issued. William's Brighton apartment was searched, as was his Mayfair home where his housekeeper had allowed Metropolitan Police access. No-one had heard from him at his club.

More death threats continued to arrive in his post box. And even though the pathologist had established the cause of death of the three kitchen staff, they were no closer to finding a killer.

Barcley was beginning to panic. Had they been abducted? Were their bodies weighted down and lying at the bottom of a lake?

He didn't think to contact Claire, who would not have divulged any helpful information anyway.

CHAPTER 22

Robin had been to Venice once before for three days as an 11 year-old with her parents. She remembered little as Giorgio, William's driver, turned the boat from Tronchetto into the Grand Canal at Piazzale Roma. Obviously, they were taking the grand entrance. She wondered whether William ever drove himself and remembered, guiltily, that she'd commandeered his driver, all those years before, when she'd stormed out of the restaurant on him, leaving him stranded. That, unfortunately, was her last memory of him until his recent return from Australia.

The ugliness of Ferrovia – the iron road – Station at Fondamenta S. Lucia was quickly replaced by the bustle of Campo S. Marcuola and, on the right, the imposing Ca' Pesaro, now a modern art gallery. But even this was dwarfed by the beauty of Ca' D'Oro, the 'golden' house, on their left. Across from Ca' D'Oro was the Rialto Mercato, now busy as traders prepared their stalls with that morning's fresh deliveries. Rounding the corner, Robin was suddenly confronted by the majestic Rialto bridge. She gasped. And on it went: Campo S. Silvestro; S. Toma, with the Frari Church looming behind it; Ca' Foscari, now the dormant university whose students had yet to rise from their beds; and finally, larger than all the other *palazzi*, Ca' Rezzonico, their destination.

They docked here, at the vaporetto stop, as William explained that his 'modest' apartment lay just behind this huge building, in which Robert Browning had died.

Nonna was all William had promised, and more. They had climbed the two flights of stairs to the apartment in the Calle de la Botteghe in Dorsoduro where the door was flung wide and the short woman, built like a heavyweight wrestler, with thick, peppered, wiry hair tied back in a bun, lifted William off the ground in a bear hug that might have crushed him were it not for the fact that she immediately released him and enveloped Robin in her sturdy arms, kissed her on the lips, and whispered in her ear in clipped English: 'You must be the one. He never bring a girl here before.'

'You can speak in Italian, Nonna. She talks like a native.'

'*Vero?*'

'No. He lies,' said Robin. 'I can just about get by.'

'Let me see you both. Such a pretty couple. But come, I have made *prima colazione*.'

It was over two hours later, when both had eaten their fill of breakfast of eggs, fried mushrooms and tomatoes and toast, that Nonna left to go back to her own modest home in Castello. Nonna was a native Venetian.

William's apartment was immaculate: the small hallway opened, on the left, onto a kitchen with a table and two chairs at one end and a laundry with a toilet and shower at the other. To the right, a formal dining room/lounge gave way, again on the right, to a large bedroom and, to the left behind the laundry area, a second, smaller bedroom. The bedrooms and lounge had tall windows looking out to identical windows across the narrow *calle* and, likewise, the kitchen was similarly overlooked. The whole place was simply, but exquisitely, furnished and the walls were covered in stunning pictures: a large Boldini portrait of what looked like two high-class prostitutes seated outside a Roman café dominated the lounge. Elsewhere, pictures of great age adorned the other rooms. Robin was later to learn that they included a Bassano *Madonna and Child*, a Gentile Bellini portrait, a Domenico Tiepolo sketch of the crucifixion, a small Francesco Guardi landscape and two Sebastiano Riccis, both *capriccios*. All were in exquisite condition and beautifully framed. Robin marvelled at what it must cost to insure them, let alone their value.

After Nonna had left, they unpacked. William held Robin to him by the end of the bed, and said: 'Are you ready?'

'For what?'

'To explore Venice.'

'Absolutely.'

'Shall we try to live like true Venetians?'

'I wouldn't know where to begin.'

'I shall teach you.'

'Let the lesson begin.'

And with that he undressed her and together they made intense, languorous love.

Afterwards, he said: 'Here beginneth the second lesson.'

She got the reference to Evensong in the Church of England.

'First things first: we keep nothing in the fridge except white wine. Everything must be fresh.

'There's a *vinaria* in San Margherita. We shall go and buy four two litre bottles of wine: two white, two red in reused plastic water bottles.'

'You aren't serious?'

'Just watch me.'

Crossing a tiny bridge over the canal they entered Campo San Barnaba with the impressive church on the left, now a da Vinci Museum, and eateries and bars around the periphery. The sun, now that they were out of the narrow calle, was warming the stones of the campo and the buildings about them, giving off a pleasant ambience that later in the day might send then scuttling for shade.

'And this is where Indiana Jones rose from a subterranean crypt full of bones,' said William, pointing to a circular manhole cover sunk in the middle of the campo.

'Which film?'

'No idea. Never watched them. But I was here when they were filming. I actually saw George Harrison come up out of that hole ...'

'I think you mean Harrison Ford. George Harrison was a Beatle.'

'Oh.'

They moved through Barnaba to San Margherita and on to the far left-hand corner. And just before the imposing church of the Carmini Friars was the *vinaria*.

William greeted Stefano, the proprietor, like a long-lost friend: a kiss on both cheeks. They spoke in hurried Italian to each other.

William left the wine, poured via plastic tubes from four of the 20 barrels lining the walls, each tagged in large letters with the name of the grape of the wine within the barrel, with Stefano as they made their way to the Carmini.

'Are you really going to drink wine delivered by tube and poured from plastic bottles?' Robin was shocked.

'It's the most quaffable wine on earth, you'll see.'

'There's something I want to show you.' William was excited.

'Why did I not understand when you were speaking with Stefano just now?'

'Ah ...'

'You were speaking *Veneziano*, weren't you?'

Veneziano is the guttural dialect spoken only by natives of Venice. It is almost unheard-of for any bar native Venetians to speak it. And most Italians can't understand it.

'Ah … yes. Well, it's easy once you get the hang of it.'

Robin realised that there were facets to this man she'd not yet imagined.

Once inside the church, he took her to the central nave aisle. There, he faced the high altar, bowed his head, and made the sign of the cross, as if this was perfectly normal.

More facets, she thought.

And just as she was about to ask him about his religious commitment, he took her hand again and almost dragged her between the heavy, deep brown pews, to a picture halfway along the nave.

It was dark, too many coats of varnish, she assumed, and set in a muted frame whose gilding needed serious attention.

But as she looked further she could feel herself overcome by its simple, un-alloyed beauty. It was perfect. Although four figures in a landscape, there was barely any background to speak of, pushing the figures forward in sharp relief. Or was she being drawn towards them? The figures composed an almost perfect triangle, its apex being the virgin's face, the Christ-child on her left shoulder. On her right, Joseph kneeling, as if in adoration and at her feet, to the left, a playful John the Baptist, only slightly older than Jesus, looking down at his antics. The scene is both familiar but nothing that might be called mundane; there's a numinous quality to it and she couldn't determine whether that arose from the composition, the artist's handling of the paint or the simple beauty of the family depicted, in the Galilee, she assumed.

'It's a Veronese, *Sacra Famiglia con S. Giovannino*,' he said. 'And look, here it is, occupying a humble position, not well-lit, with no crowds jostling to see it. What a privilege we enjoy!

'This is one of the many reasons I love Venice: every hundred yards or so, there's a church. And in those many churches are literally thousands of masterpieces by some of the greatest painters the world has ever known. Just hanging quietly and unpretentiously on grubby walls like this, offering us glimpses of heaven.

'Here, surely, is the highest concentration of high art known to the world.'

Robin, moved to tears, held his face in her hands, and gently kissed his lips.

They picked up their wine, stowed it in the fridge and headed back out.

'If we're going to live like the natives, we need to cook seriously. And to do that we need fresh produce. I said there'd be nothing in the fridge but white wine ... That's because first thing in the morning, we'll walk to *Impronta* for *cappuccini e brioche con crema* ... and, possibly, a prosecco.'

'I'll get fat ... and besides, you only drink Americanos.'

'Not in Venice ... and then we'll go to Campo San Stefano where there is a daily outdoor market or, preferably, to Rialto where we can get all the meat and veg. we want. There's a magnificent *pescaria* there as well. And an unusual *macelleria*!'

'You mean we'll eat horse?'

'Of course. This is Venice.'

Because it was nearing lunchtime, they decided to eat in an *osteria*. William had already booked a restaurant for dinner that evening; they would start their food shopping tomorrow.

They caught a *vaporetto* No. 2 from Ca' Rezzonico, retracing their earlier path in William's boat in reverse, and alighted at San Stae. The destination was Osteria Mocenigo, one of William's favourite Venetian eateries.

Robin detected a change in William: it was as if all the turmoil of recent days had evaporated and a calmer, happier William had emerged, unscathed by the threat of death.

And yet, given the insights she'd gleaned in only the last few hours, she was wary of being too confident that she knew this man that well, or that their troubles lay behind them, back in England.

That evening, they ate at *Il Squero*, a small restaurant with only 15 covers, in Calle Toletta, not far from their apartment.

Again, William was greeted like a long-lost friend and immediately they were seated, two Bellinis appeared before them: Robin's idea of heaven. The night was still warm as they sat looking through the open windows onto the Ponte Squero – a small, exquisitely-formed bridge - and the steady stream of passers-by.

It was easy, in this different world, to put their minds to what mattered: a burgeoning love in both their hearts.

CHAPTER 23

The Accademia, one of the world's finest art galleries, was a 200-yard walk from William's apartment. Its renown was based on the fact that it was the repository of some of the finest Renaissance art the world has known: the Bellinis, Titian, Veronese, Tintoretto, Giorgione, Bassano, del Piombo, the Tiepolos ... were here in abundance. And of that cornucopia of treasures, at its heart, was Giorgione's *La Tempesta*.

Not long ago perfectly restored, and in pride of place, *La Tempesta* was one of the few acknowledged paintings by Giorgione, at the height of his powers. Yet the picture remained a puzzle.

Born in 1477/8 in Castelfranco in the Veneto, Giorgione was, in William's rather idiosyncratic view, the greatest painter of the Venetian High Renaissance, eclipsing even Titian, Tintoretto and Giorgione's own erstwhile teacher Giovanni Bellini. He died of the plague, a little over thirty years of age, in 1510. For William, his work had an elusive, almost poetic, quality. And this was further pronounced by the fact that of the dozens of works purporting to be by him, only six could make his *catalogue raisonné*.

Of his six known paintings, *La Tempesta* is the most enigmatic. Some have suggested that it is the first landscape in the history of Western painting.

The picture portrays, in the foreground on the left, a soldier, and over a stream, on the right, a breast-feeding woman. Trees frame the town beyond them and above them all, a storm brews. The mystery of the painting has led to many suggested meanings: a work without subject; the first *capriccio* of Venetian art; Adam and Eve expelled from the Garden of Eden; the finding of the baby Moses; the figures of Charity and Fortitude; the birth of Paris; an alchemical scene; a metaphor of the taking of Padua during the War of Cambrai; an allusion to the Vendramin and the taking of Chioggia.

William had studied all these possibilities and more and yet was unconvinced. For him it was one of the finest pieces of sixteenth century landscape painting: despite the sky being dense with dark, distended clouds and a streak of lightning, people, objects and buildings stand out with the greatest, magical, optical clarity. Although he didn't like the notion of having favourites, it was his favourite picture. He had, over the years, the growing suspicion that it was a 'literary' painting; that it was a romantic symbol: 'Thee as in my mortal frame I lov'd, so loos'd forth it I love thee still,' from Dante's second Canto in *Purgatorio*. Or possibly a reference from Homer.

William had long dreamed that he might find the clue to its symbolism.

He was still explaining the possibilities to Robin when an attendant gently suggested that they'd spent more than enough time in front of the Accademia's most famous painting and that it was time to give other people a chance to look at it.

Covered in embarrassment, and realizing that he'd been lost in the majestic mystery of this most glorious of pictures, William apologized and moved away quickly.

Again, and not for the first time that day, Robin marvelled at the breadth of William's interests and the depth of his feeling for things of beauty.

CHAPTER 24

Sam Wilson, bereft of information because as ignorant as his police source, filled his column with lurid speculation about William and Robin's whereabouts. But most of his articles were designed to titillate his readers with tales enlarging the threat facing them both. The extremist past of the two *Persons of Interest*, who had threatened William's life, and had been arrested, were poured over in relished detail.

The fact that the autopsy of the three kitchen staff revealed that aconite had been used as the instrument of death, sent Wilson scurrying through the corridors of the internet in search of other such poisonings.

He clumsily noted that it was no coincidence that a Sunni cleric in Saudi Arabia had been poisoned using the same substance, suggesting Sh'ia involvement. Maybe William and Robin were caught in the crosshairs of internecine Islamic warfare, he concluded and in so doing defied both the evidence available and logic.

But reason had never been Wilson's strong suit and sensationalism sold papers, so who worried?

Even staid, broadsheet newspapers took up the story, adding sensation to speculation. The BBC TV ran a fourth slot item on 'Where are they now?' saying that the police urged the public to contact New Scotland Yard with any information of the whereabouts of William Adams and Robin Atwell. The switchboards at New Scotland Yard were flooded.

◆ ◆ ◆

James Southwell was stymied. William Adams had not been into the Institute for over a week now, and that was unlike him. He'd rung Oriel, but the porter had told him that Professor Adams 'is away'. And was unwilling to give further information. In fact, he was acting on police instructions.

All became clear when a junior researcher knocked sheepishly on his door and showed him a copy of *The Mail*, opened to the column *Oxford Intrigues*, by Sam Wilson.

'I thought you might like to see this, Professor,' she said, knowing full-well that such a notable as the Director of the Taylor Institute would never stoop to reading a rag like *The Mail*. Southwell was shocked to see the headline: 'William Adams Disappears'.

Wilson's stooge in the Thames Valley Police had, for a tidy sum, leaked the news to him.

Wilson speculated on where Adams and his girlfriend, 'the stunning Oxford beauty' Dr Robin Atwell, might have gone.

Against the expectations of his staff, Southwell cut out the article and posted it on the staff notice board; this was so unlike him. Clearly he was worried.

CHAPTER 25

An older email with a utility bill for Calle de le Botteghe, from Nonna Claudia to Claire, gave him the address he needed. He had already intercepted their travel plans from Claire's email correspondence with William. And now he knew where in Venice they would be staying.

He'd not been to Venice before so, with typical and deliberate execution, he planned his trip to *La Serenissima*.

He could not afford a long absence. He would not draw attention to himself thus. But he could travel there and back at the weekends of which, given Adams and Claire's correspondence, he reckoned he had at least three.

An easyJet return leaving inconveniently at 22.00 from Gatwick got him to Marco Polo airport at 23.30 local time. The No. 5 bus from the airport deposited him at Piazzale Roma, across the long bridge from the mainland and beyond which no cars could go. From there he would, duffel bag over his shoulder, walk the short distance to his Air B&B in Campo Carita, a ten-minute stroll from Adams' apartment.

He would use this weekend to plan his attack. His false passport, purchased on the dark web, should arrive any day now.

CHAPTER 26

While not yet the height of summer, it was still pleasantly warm and the city was thronged with tourists.

Their lives easily fell into a pattern: they rose as the light coming through their bedroom shutters was sufficiently bright to make dozing no longer easy. A delightful, gentle way to wake, William decided.

Usually, after ablutions, they made love. Then they would make their way to market, more often than not to Rialto, to purchase that day's provisions; they decided on the way what they would eat that day. But first, always breakfast at *Impronta* – standing at the bar, as Venetians did – *due cappuccini: una decaffeinato e una normale e due brioche con crema, per favore*. The two girls behind the counter could recite the order before they reached the bar. They got to know them both quite well. Luciana was studying law at Foscari, Venice's university, morning shifts at *Impronta* only, and Julia was full-time. They decided she was 'on the scale', mild Asberger's, they thought. Both girls were an ebullient, friendly delight.

Quite often, just before the market, they would stop at Calle Toscana for a prosecco or, in William's case, a *caffè corretto*, and then to buy their fish or meat and produce from the teeming, smelly, noise-filled markets.

For the next two weeks they spent their days exploring the city. But as time went by William, equipped with a tiny folding chair, a man-bag of fine black ink pens and pencils, and a moleskin sketchbook, would find a spot to sketch: every corner turned provided a new vista; vignettes of beautiful cityscape unparalleled elsewhere: Ponte Pugni, Rio San Barnaba, Fondamenta Alberti, Arsenale, Instituto Veneto di Scienza Lettere e d'Arti. His best sketch was Il Masquero in Santa Maria Formosa, an ugly face in stone, set into the wall of the church to ward off evil spirits.

As William sketched, Robin increasingly spent time in the Liberia Sansoviniana preparing the bare bones for a book she was thinking of writing: *The Impact of Early Roman Law on Mediaeval Venetian Tort*.

After lunch, usually cooked by William, they would have their siesta and again make love before setting out mid-afternoon.

Dinner they often ate out: the Danieli, the Gritti, the Cipriani occasionally, but often at ristoranti and osteria favoured by the locals: *La Bitta "NO FISH!"*, just around the corner from them; *alla Staffa* near the mighty church of SS. Giovanni e Paolo; and *Crea* on Guidecca, *specialità veneziane di pesce*.

If there was a concert or opera on offer, they did their best to attend, and this they could manage most nights.

CHAPTER 27

Early on, they established the habit of taking pre-dinner drinks on the Zattere, the long esplanade ranging from the Dogana at the Bacino to Tronchetto. From here they could look across the Canal of the same name to Guidecca, the southern-most island of Venice proper.

From Calle de le Botteghe they strolled in the evening warmth to Fondamenta Sangiatoffetti, past the Liceo Artistico Statale and then, on their right, the church of San Trovaso with its imposing tower and identical West and North façades and its glorious Tintoretto *Ultima Cena* in a transept; past the Squero, Venice's one remaining boat yard, still making and repairing gondolas, and finally turning left onto the Zattere where sat *Chez Nico*, not simply one of the many bars near their apartment, but also the best *gelataria* in Venice.

'You can always tell,' said William. 'The best banana ice cream is always grey …'

Robin thought better than to question the wisdom of this.

After ordering their drinks, an Aperol spritz for Robin and a Campari spritz for William, together with a bowl of crisps and one of olives, they would weave their way through the inevitable horde of tourists to the waterside of the fondamenta to watch the passing traffic: car boats to the Lido, passenger ferries and the busy vaporetti on their way from the Zattere to San Giorgio or Redentore – the two Guidecca masterpieces by Palladio –

Zitelle and Palanca.

But the main objects of interest were the cruise ships. Almost daily, one or more of these hideous monsters, dragged by two tugs, would force their way down the Guidecca Canal creating untold damage to foundations, quaysides and infrastructure while their passengers stood, inevitably, in their bathrobes on their balconies, waving to the locals. Doubtless they mistook the one-fingered riposte from those on the shore as a return greeting. Robin found herself joining William in his angry gesticulation, along with all the natives present, to these thoughtless interlopers.

Occasionally, they would forgo *Chez Nico* to go to *Cantine del Vino gli Schiavi*, the favourite watering hole of Commissario Brunetti, Donna Leon's fictional detective, whose novels William enjoyed while staying in Venice. Here, the *cicchetti* – snacks and sandwiches - were among the best in town, and the priciest. Their morning food shopping and their evening drinks were the constants in their otherwise varied days. Robin believed she was getting a feel for the place when something happened that determined they should return to England.

CHAPTER 28

His first visit to Venice was a success. The Air B&B he'd taken was a mere ten minutes from Adams' apartment.

He'd arrived near midnight and was relieved to get the second-to-last No. 5 bus from Marco Polo airport to Piazzale Roma. Once there, he'd thrown his rucksack over his shoulder and found his accommodation, twenty minutes later, with relative ease: the streets were empty but well-lit, casting long shadows, and his map was easy to follow.

Because he only had the weekend to get his mission underway, he rose early on the Saturday morning and walked to the heart of Dorsoduro to scout the area around Adams' apartment.

Already, at six o'clock in the morning, it was warm and the city was beginning to stir. Noisy rubbish barges with large, centrally placed mechanical claws, removed copious metal bins, spilling their contents into the boat. Black plastic sacks from pavements of the mostly narrow calli were thrown into one of the two large maws which fed the cavernous belly of the boat. Teams of two cleared the streets with remarkable efficiency, the begloved man on foot gingerly picking up the bags marked *vetro* to be placed in the second hole of the boat, specifically there for glass. The whole exercise was rackety, quick and business-like. *If only things were so well-ordered at home*, he thought.

So engrossed was he in the rubbish operation that he

almost failed to notice Adams and the woman emerge from Sotoportego e calle Pedrocchi, the alleyway behind Calle de le Botteghe, which obviously was the actual entrance to the apartment. His plans would have been shot had they noticed him and God only knows what he would have said if they'd caught him lingering around their flat. He chided himself: he hadn't come this far, gone to so much trouble and expense, and killed three innocent people into the bargain, only to be caught flat-footed now.

It was 8.00am and the streets were starting to fill with Venetians doing their daily food shopping and tourists fumbling their way around the intricate pattern of water-lined streets in gawping awe.

The crowds provided ample cover as he followed them north, he knew not where.

They crossed a large campo past a church with a faded sign identifying it as San Pantalon. (He made a mental note: when this was all over, he must return to examine these treasures at his leisure.) Then they ducked into a bar, announcing itself as *Impronta* in large letters above the door. He panicked. He couldn't walk past them for fear of being seen. If he remained where he was and they returned the way they had come he would be spotted. If he moved out of range, he ran the risk of losing them. What to do?

A small coffee shop was just opening behind him. If they were having a morning coffee then they should be no longer than ten minutes or so; breakfast, at least double that. He ducked into the café, realising that his lack of Italian might impede his ability to carry out his mission as best he might wish.

Sitting two tables along from the front, opposite the bar, he realized that he would not see them pass unless they came back the way they had arrived and his plans would be ruined. If he lost them now, they might elude him all day and his attempt to establish a pattern of their movements would be thwarted.

As he considered this conundrum, he noticed, from the corner of his eye, that they sauntered past, hand-in-hand, her leaning into him, whispering what he supposed were sweet nothings to each other. It made him sick.

Realizing that he knew so little of what his mission actually entailed, he left a few euros – probably too much – on his table and gingerly made his way back out into the narrow calle. They did not turn back down the street from which they'd come but continued on, northwards, he assumed.

By now, the crowds were thickening and following them unobserved was easy, not least of which because they were so immersed in their own solipsistic bubble.

He tried to remember the route they took: Calle dei Scalater, past a church which had Frari in its name, into a large square called, he thought, Campo San Polo. He cursed his lack of preparation and his not knowing any Italian.

Eventually, they came to what he knew was the Rialto Bridge. This they by-passed and merged with the large numbers now thronging the stalls of what was a series of markets: fish, meat, vegetables, spices. On and on it went. He realized that the more he trailed them, the greater the chance of exposure and the consequent ruination of his plan. His flagging confidence was only restored by the ever-growing crowds and the fact that they seemed to take no notice of much of what went on about them, so absorbed were they in each other. It made him want to vomit.

His whole plan had been to travel to Venice over a few weekends, observe them, establish any patterns or habits of behaviour they maintained and, on the basis of that, determine the best location where he might kill Adams, preferably in front of the slut he now dragged around the dirty, smelly, fucking Italian market.

He realized that he would need to be more vigilant than he had been thus far and would need to acquaint himself more comprehensively with Venice than he had done in preparation for this visit.

It became clear to him that, after the market and with a small bag of provisions, they made their way back to his apartment, with a brief stop on the way at a bar where they both – at nine in the morning! – drank a glass of fizz.

Sunday followed a similar shape to Saturday, but was more productive. They'd followed the same pattern as the early morning before: the leisurely stroll to *Impronta*, the shopping at Rialto Mercato, the return to the flat with the provisions. Thereafter, things had changed. He'd gone off on his own, as had she. He decided, on Saturday, to follow Adams, only to discover that he'd deposited himself in a very public place, in front of a disused church called Derelitti, there to draw. He was astonished. Was his otherwise exalted life actually so infantile as to spend his time drawing?!

The'd met back at the apartment, for lunch he assumed, and had not emerged until just after three. He realised he was beginning to flag; he had underestimated the demands that simple surveillance made on one.

Again, they went their separate ways. This time, on Sunday, he followed her to what appeared to be a large library near St Mark's Square.

Both evenings, they had drinks by a large canal that overlooked what appeared to be an island opposite; they ate in a nearby restaurant on both evenings and then went home.

He was pleased to be back in his own modest Air B&B. He was exhausted. Having done nothing more than snack all day as and when their frequent stops allowed, he fell asleep, fully-clothed, without an evening meal. He was determined that his visit the following weekend would be better planned, more productive, less haphazard.

But the germ of a strategy was insinuating itself into his consciousness as he drifted off into sleep.

CHAPTER 29

As she lay one afternoon, cradled in William's arms, Robin confessed that she'd fallen in love with Venice, that she'd fallen in love with the life into which they'd fallen there and that, more vitally, she'd fallen even deeper in love with him.

For him, the guilt he at first felt when he was with Robin – guilt that he was somehow betraying Gill's memory – while not evaporated, at least had changed into a quiet confidence that Gill would not disapprove. He still thought of Gill daily, longingly and with the profound sadness he knew he would carry forever.

Sometimes the memory of her was too hard to bear. He tried, with varying degrees of success, to expunge her from his mind. But often that only compounded his guilt … and his grief.

Now, however, with Robin nestled in his arms, he felt a contented reciprocity with Gill's memory that meant, for the first time since he and Robin had come together again, he felt able to respond: 'And I love you, too.'

She held him tight, her tears pooling on his shoulder.

She took his enlarging penis, hefted herself onto one elbow and straddled him, slowly putting him into her before settling into a languid rhythm above him.

Her tears fell to his chest as she moved. Eternity and love coalesced in that moment: she knew they would be together for all time.

◆ ◆ ◆

Not a great deal smaller than a football pitch, in both size and dimensions, the *piano nobile* of the Scuola Grande di San Rocco was, in William's mind, the most glorious room on earth.

Scuole, an institution unique to Venice, are devotional lay brotherhoods answerable to the State rather than the Church. There are six *scuole*, and they are very, very rich. Of the six, the wealthiest is the Scuola Grande di San Rocco, with members drawn from the moneyed professional classes.

These confraternities, which enjoyed dressing up in their distinctive uniforms with their arcane hierarchies denoted by gold braid and shiny medals, devoted a great deal of time and expense to beautifying their meeting houses and, of the six, San Rocco was the most beautiful. Along with San Marco, San Rocco - the French plague protector St Roche - was Venice's other patron saint; his body was brought to Venice in 1485.

In 1564, the Scuola ran a competition for the School's internal decoration. Tintoretto stole a march on his rivals, Veronese included, by presenting a finished painting rather than the required sketch. In three intensive sessions over the following 23 years, Tintoretto went on to make San Rocco his masterpiece.

In addition to large paintings depicting the life of Christ on the ground floor, the *piano nobile* ceiling was painted entirely by him, offering a running commentary on Old Testament stories, along with the Albergo, where his greatest masterpiece, The Crucifixion, is to be found. William had cried when he first saw it.

William and Robin sat at the end of the fourth row of many in the grand room – listening to the music of the *Cantori Veneziani* – William quietly sketching the intricate wooden carving of Tintoretto by Pianta adorning the sedilia, just to his left. It was one statue of many: their rough-hewn beauty adding a three-dimensional, and at times mysterious, character to the paintings of Tintoretto on the ceiling above them.

He'd completed Tintoretto's face and was just about to move to the outline, including the artist's pot of paintbrushes when, from nowhere he'd later be able to identify, it came to him: the first anonymous note was directed at him personally. From memory, he scribbled down the note again:

MET = ES & HG

CL.E.VER. BUT...

It was not about the Metropolitan Police, nor was 'HG' Hamish Grant. The note spoke of his greatest achievement, of his finally achieving his intellectual ambition: to decipher the uncracked language of Meroitic. He'd managed this four years before, in Babylon, working in a bell tent with Ellie, slaving over a stela with two identical inscriptions: the top in Egyptian hieroglyphs – his own area of expertise – and the bottom in Meroitic, also written using the Egyptian alphabet.

Translating the top inscription had led to his ability to decipher the bottom and thus to unravel the mysterious language of Meroitic. Not since Michael Ventris had managed to interpret the Minoan Linear B language had anyone made such a monumental achievement.

And not only did it establish William's place in the Hall of Fame of linguists, it confirmed his hitherto now much published theory that Meroitic was, in fact, the grammar and syntax of the other languages of the Sahel – Berber, Gallo and Tuareg – imposed on the alphabet of the North, of Egypt. In other words, the Hamitic grammar of Africa was melded with the Semitic script of Egypt.

Under his scribbled reproduction of the first half of the death threat he wrote:

ES & HG

E = Egyptian

S = script (or Semitic)

& = and

H = Hamitic

G = grammar

MET, he assumed, therefore had to mean 'Meroitic'. It was either deliberately mis-written to confuse or was simply a common example of many elided words given in short-hand. So:

Meroitic = Egyptian script and Hamitic grammar. A concise description of his discovery.

The rest of the note then fell into place: CL.E.VER was another misdirection: it wasn't Larry's initials, it simply meant 'clever', an understatement when it came to William's crowning achievement.

The second note confirmed: YOU'RE GOING TO DIE. The only conclusion possible was, therefore, that precisely because he'd discovered that Meroitic was the imposition of Hamitic grammar on Egyptian script, he was going to be killed. But why?

Why would anyone want to make a death threat about a linguistic discovery, no matter how monumental?

Robin had noticed that he'd given over sketching in favour of something else and soon realised that he was rewriting the death threat.

Her brows furrowed as a look of alarm took hold of her. She took his hand, shrugged her shoulders as if to say 'what?!' then looked to him for a reply.

There was nothing for it but for them to leave the concert immediately. Unfortunately, this meant walking back twenty or so rows, then behind the width of the audience, then down the opposite side, coming almost level with the orchestra still playing furiously and some giving them disapproving looks, then down the long flight of stairs with Tintoretto's plague scenes facing them, admonishing, from the walls of the staircase, and into the grand ground floor with each of Tintoretto's characters from scenes of Jesus' life staring at them accusingly, and then out into the balmy Campo.

They stood there, facing each other, by the steps of the adjacent Chiesa San Rocco, as William explained what he'd found.

Robin was alarmed at William's reaction to the discovery and although she was certain, now that he explained it, that he was correct, she was at a loss: 'What are we to do?'

CHAPTER 30

While the discovery of the meaning of the note materially changed nothing, it changed everything.

The decision to return was not easy: they'd both come to love their Italian way of life. But it was more than that. Robin relished her quiet, unforced research in the Liberia, while William realized that he enjoyed his sketching as much as he did working on the *Lexicon*. And what's more, he was becoming quite good at it. As he sat on his little fold-up chair, his knees up around his chest, the sketchbook precariously balanced on one knee, passers-by, invariably, would stop, peer over his shoulder and comment on his craftsmanship. Two women, both American tourists, had used the opportunity as a chat-up line.

It wasn't just that Robin's time was running out, but they decided that William's decipherment might give the hitherto floundering police investigation focus. Barcley would see just how pertinent this new insight was and fresh lines of enquiry could therefore be pursued.

Their jet was in the air and would arrive at Marco Polo at about midday. They said their farewells to Nonna who squeezed Robin so hard she struggled to wriggle free.

Giorgio drove them up the Grand Canal, towards Piazzale Roma, the reverse of the trip they'd made on their arrival. Robin tried, but failed, to hide her tears from William as they sailed under the Rialto Bridge, then she smiled as she remembered that William had told her that the bridge had been built by Signore da Ponte, who'd won a competition to design it, beating Michelangelo in the process: the bridge built by Mister Bridge. Her reluctance to leave was only ameliorated by the fact that the man standing next to her, his arm around her waist, the man she'd loved since she foolishly pushed him away, was now committed to her in a love so tangible it almost ached. In spite of her sadness at their departure, she'd never been so happy.

◆ ◆ ◆

They returned to William's rooms just before six, Barcley waiting outside for them, as arranged. His anger at their unannounced disappearance was quickly dissipated by Robin's charm and a double gin. They settled in the panelled drawing room, a Laura Knight oil hanging on the wall behind Barcley.

'I think I've managed to unravel our notes,' said William.

'Oh, yes …' said Barcley, tentative and unsure about whether he shouldn't be angry at not having been told about this earlier. But as Robin, who somehow appeared to him to be different, smiled at him, his anger melted away.

'Yes,' said William. 'I've written it out for you.' And with that he handed Barcley a sheet of paper, William's interpretation of the note written in full:

MET = ES & HG

CL.E.VER. BUT …

YOU'RE GOING TO DIE

Meroitic = Egyptian script plus Hamitic grammar

Clever. But …

You're going to die.

It might as well have been in Greek, which, from their previous encounters, he knew William could read.

'I'm afraid I'm none the wiser,' he said.

'It's quite straightforward if you're familiar with my discovery: there's an African language called Meroitic, named after a town called Meroë between the fifth and sixth cataracts of the Nile; it was the capital of the Kingdom of Nubia in ancient times. The language was written using the Egyptian alphabet and, until four years ago, it had never been deciphered ...'

'And you cracked it?'

'Yes.'

'I vaguely remember reading something about it in the papers.'

By now Barcley had finished his gin and Robin rose, taking all their glasses, to replenish them.

'Right. Well ... it was a stroke of fortune, actually,' said William, when in fact it was a stroke of genius. 'When I was in Babylon, we discovered this stela – a large, carved rock made of basalt – with two sets of writing on it. At the top: Egyptian, and underneath, what turned out to be Meroitic.

I was able to use the top inscription to work out what the bottom meant and so I managed, with a lot of luck, to crack the language.'

'It had nothing to do with luck,' Robin interrupted from the drinks cabinet. 'It was sheer brilliance.'

'Right ... oh ... er,' William stumbled at Robin's praise. 'Anyway, I'd already been working on Meroitic for several years, using various inscriptions from all over Nubia.

'And here's the relevant bit: my thesis was that Meroitic was Hamitic syntax and grammar...'

'Hermetic?'

'Oh, sorry, the languages of the Sahel ... Essentially, native African languages, this structure of these languages formed the basis of Meroitic but using the Egyptian alphabet.

'And as it transpired, the stela proved I was right.'

'So …?'

'So that's what the note means: if you add Egyptian alphabet, or script, the S, to Hamitic grammar, HG, you get Meroitic. And whoever wrote the note thought that was clever,' he trailed off.

'ES and HG I think I understand. But how does MET equal Meroitic? And why the full stop after the CL and E?'

'Both are designed to mislead.'

'And this is worth killing you for!?' Barcley was incredulous.

'Well, I must confess, that's the part I really don't understand. You see, if I'm right then the only motive for the death threat can be some kind of professional jealousy.'

'I suppose people have been killed for less,' said Barcley doubtfully.

'Nonetheless, I'm confident that's what the note means,' William offered.

'So you cracked this language. You beat your rivals to it. And one of them, in a fit of jealousy, not only threatens to kill you for it, but mistakenly kills three people in the process. Is that what you're saying?'

'Yes. That's *just* what I'm saying.'

'So, how many people did you beat to get this language cracked?'

'Two.'

'What!!?'

'Yes. Just two, as far as I'm aware.'

'Well, that narrows it down, I suppose.'

'I'm afraid that may not make things all that much easier.'

'Why?'

'Because one is in Australia, at the Australian National University, and the other is at Notre Dame, in Indiana in the US.'

Robin could see the look of stupefaction on Barcley's face. Without asking, she took his glass to refill it for a third time.

'Better make that my last,' he said. 'My brain is fuzzy enough as it is.'

As she made the drink, she explained, giving William some respite, 'All of these languages are really quite difficult ...'

'I suppose that's why they've not been cracked until lately,' offered the detective.

'Quite right. And it's all in a pretty arcane and esoteric field. There weren't that many people who dedicated their lives to breaking the code behind Meroitic. And probably more importantly, universities are mostly not willing to fund the research necessary. It's just not sexy, like, say, quantum mechanics ...' Robin realised she might be disappearing down the rabbit hole so she brought things back to reality. 'Anyway, the academic community in this obscure field of Meroitic ...'

William spluttered into his gin. '... into this field is very small. The academics all know each other; they all publish their articles in the same, small number of journals and they all correspond with each other.

'But, deep down, there is academic rivalry and, yes, there are jealousies.

'William's colleagues, the only two men we are aware were working on the language, were Professor Lansdale at ANU and Dr Christodoulos at Notre Dame.

'If William is right about what that note means, then they would be the obvious candidates.'

'But, of course, there may be other academics of whom I'm unaware, although I think that unlikely,' said William.

'And there might be amateurs,' said Robin. 'Mavericks working on their own, not engaged with the academic community. Although that seems unlikely too.'

Barcley had had enough. He wanted to go home and go to sleep.

William wrote down the names and contact numbers of the two he'd mentioned and undertook to provide Barcley with any further pertinent information should that arise.

As he was leaving, Barcley turned, put his foot in the door, and looking stiffly at them both, said, 'And don't leave town without letting me know.'

'Yes, of course, Inspector,' they chimed.

CHAPTER 31

Their return from Venice had been difficult for both of them. They'd grown into an easy, relaxed pattern of life where they could do as they pleased, without any threat hanging over their heads, and where they revelled in the beauty of the city: the paintings, the architecture, the light, the music, the food.

Turning every unfamiliar corner was a new vista, often of great beauty, a new adventure, an undiscovered painting, occasionally of transcendent purity, even when it was Saint Lucia, her eyes plucked out by Roman persecutors and sitting incongruously on a pristine plate, painted by Tiepolo for the church of San Geremia. Or Fumiani's powerful Christ Scourging the Temple Merchants in Chiesa San Rocco. Or, William's favourite, Titian's Assumption of the Blessed Virgin in the Frari.

And although Oxford, too, had its beauties; although it, too, drew tourists to throng its streets, it lacked the charm and the self-assurance of Venice. Doubtless, William mused, its inheritance from a time when *La Serenissima* ruled Europe.

University and college commitments made demands on both of them. Robin, in particular, had to set aside work on her book, while William fell back into the pattern of almost daily research on his *Lexicon*.

In this respect, Jack Sutherland had become a godsend: whenever William had consulted him on this word or that,

Jack, sometimes without hesitation, more often after a day or two's research, would return to William with new sources, cross-references to existing texts or new avenues for consideration. It often seemed to William that, whenever he went to Jack for help, Jack would drop whatever of his own work that he was doing, in order to concentrate – selflessly and generously – on William's research.

Increasingly, William found himself relying on Jack, so much so that he considered offering him the chance of co-authorship. And while he finally rejected that option, it was obvious that Jack's contribution would need to be acknowledged in the most generous terms. He clearly shared William's enthusiasm for the *Lexicon*. And while this no doubt would enhance his own work in the history of Meroë and Napatan, Jack's assiduousness in his support of the *Lexicon* was manifestly not motivated for selfish reasons alone.

More pleasingly for William, he felt that Jack was becoming a friend.

◆ ◆ ◆

While William's rooms in Oriel were ideal for a bachelor academic, it was plain that with the two of them now sharing the space, they would soon need to find something larger, not least three-bedroom, so that William and Robin could have a study each: at present they shared the same work room and Robin's expansive, not to say chaotic, method of filing notes and drafts, meant that, inevitably, they were falling over each other's feet.

William enlisted Claire's help in finding a house in Summertown. A task she undertook with relish.

Summertown, the posh residential end of Oxford, was well-serviced by plenty of shops and restaurants and quiet streets lined with substantial Victorian properties which were, a generation ago, favoured by dons, but now well beyond most academics' reach financially.

Claire started her search in Northmore Road – Oxford's most expensive – or thereabouts. She relished visiting houses on William's behalf. She enjoyed even more the frisson of pleasure when ill-informed estate agents mistook her for William's partner.

CHAPTER 32

It was not long after their return that William and Robin's presence in Oxford made its way into Sam Wilson's column with a hint, provided by Wilson's source in the Thames Valley Police, that they had done so because Prof William Adams, the man who had cracked not one language but two, had managed to unpack the riddle of the death threat notes.

The effect of Wilson's perorations was to galvanise those who found Adams' life's work an abomination into actual plans to kill him.

Mohammed al Farabi and his brother Waheed, were *Persons of Interest*. They had committed no crime. They had broken no law. But the CTB, the counter-terrorism branch of the Metropolitan Police, had decided, in spite of budgets stretched to breaking point, to put them under surveillance because of their interest – one desk sergeant had called it a 'fetish' - with the internet jihadi activity of Islamic State and, in particular, with mutilations, beheadings, immolations and other instruments of punishment for sins against the Prophet, peace be upon him. They took an especial interest in hangings in Raqqah and Mosul, when the Caliphate was at its apotheosis: cherry-pickers used as makeshift scaffolds from which long nooses were suspended, the thief or idolater or adulterer dangling obscenely for hours on end *pour encourager les autres*.

The brothers' daily visits to heterosexual porn sites were of little significance compared with the depravity of their Islamist trawling.

Surveillance of Mohammed and Waheed was, given the financial constraints under which the CTB laboured, cursory: two men operating daytime shifts only, in addition to the standard, automated monitoring of their online activity, which occurred at all hours.

But with the publication of Sam Wilson's *Oxford Intrigues* column in *The Mail*, Mohammed and Waheed's internet activity took an interesting turn. Their attention shifted to research into the life of the world's most famous archaeologist: of his notoriety in Babylon; of the *fatwa* against him, announced by ISIS once he'd deciphered an uncracked language and translated a pagan cylinder; of the successful ISIS attacks on the dig site in Babylon, leading to the closure of the excavation and the deaths of many infidels. And on it went.

Wilson's column provided a blow-by-blow itinerary of William Adams' life, together with his adulterous relationship with his fellow academic. And in this Mohammed and Waheed showed undue interest. They seemed particularly interested in which of their brothers it was who had attempted to murder the infidel using poison.

The number of case officers rose from two to eight as the fetish became an infatuation and the CTB began to worry for Professor William Adams' safety.

◆ ◆ ◆

Mohammed could not remember his mother. She had left the family not long after Waheed's birth, bound for the peace and security of home in rural Pakistan. She could no longer bear the depredations of her appalling husband: the beatings, his laziness, his bigotry and, worst of all, his arrogance. In the end, she decided that the only thing about which he might rightly be arrogant was that he was male. And that was not only not enough, but it was precisely the reason she could not stay any longer to raise her cherished Mohammed and his newly infant brother Waheed.

Osama al Farabi was as caring a father as he was as devoted a husband. The boys were brought up largely by their aunt whose affection for them ranged between desultory and strained. Their school attendance and its enforcement was haphazard and their relationships, beyond family, extended only so far as the local mosque, and these were strictly male only.

Like their father, both boys were arrogant and plug ugly, the only hope of female companionship would depend on a marriage arranged on tribal lines. They'd also inherited his disdain for women whose only function, in his view, was to serve and service the better half of the species. And, like their father, at 22 and 21, they had never done a day's work: beneficiaries of the state's incompetently distributed munificence.

It was thus that Mohammed and Waheed grew up in their two-up, two-down council house in the seediest part of Bradford; ill-educated, hating women, angry that life had not blessed them as they deserved, and brimming with resentment. The only two things about which they felt passionate were religion, which was a different iteration of resentment directed at those who failed to share the Prophet's dogmatism, and sex, fuelled by pornography with masturbation as the only outlet: they were too poor to pay for it.

Mohammed had initiated the daily ritual in the closet-like bedroom they shared, their two single beds wedged against opposite walls with little space left to manoeuvre between them. He chose his porn for the day on his laptop, the sound turned to a bare minimum and, facing the wall, away from Waheed, brought himself to an unsatisfying climax, during which he whispered *Allahu Akbar*, into a filthy handkerchief saved for just that purpose.

Waheed followed his older brother's example on the bed opposite.

Of late, Mohammed had taken to masturbating to the pictures of Robin Atwell he'd conjured up on his screen from the newspaper and television reports. He would dream at night of himself doing it to her, again and again, and shared his dreams with Waheed, encouraging him to do the same. In fact, he suggested, they could both have her at the same time: one from the front, one from behind.

This fantasy, pored over in detail in their limited imaginations, led to a growing resentment of the man who actually did it to her, and formed the incipient plan to punish him for his presumption: he clearly deserved to suffer, and the earlier ISIS *fatwa* only served to confirm their decision, brewed over many weeks, to kill him and, having raped her – one from the front, one from behind – to kill her also.

Should they be caught in their efforts, then better still. Should they be martyred in attempting the *fatwa*, then they would enjoy the greatest heavenly bliss available: never-ending sex in the arms of the 72 black-eyed *houris*.

Mohammed had found a website: *A Martyr's Reward*, which explained in pornographic detail, the teachings of the Hadith. Although mentioned in the Qu'ran, the *houris* are described at length in the Hadith, a collection of sayings of the Prophet, peace be upon him, regarded as scripture.

The *houris* are virgins with beautiful eyes who are a reward for the faithful in paradise. They are composed of saffron from feet to knees, of musk from knees to breasts, of amber from breasts to neck, and of camphor from neck to head. With their 'swelling breasts' they recline on red hyacinth couches embedded with rubies and jewels. They do not urinate or defecate or sleep, do not get pregnant, do not menstruate and are never sick. They are hairless, except for eyebrows and head. At 33 years-old, they are eternally young and eternally available. They live for no other purpose than the sexual satisfaction of the faithful martyrs and their virginity is renewed after each copulation. And, in Mohammed's imagination, he cherished the hope that each of the 72 was an only slightly different iteration of Robin Atwell.

What more, thought the brothers, could a man of faith want?

CHAPTER 33

Try as he might, William had not been able to get a hold of Larry Verity. There was no answer on his phone, at his apartment, or via his pigeon-hole in the Porters' Lodge; he had, it appeared, vanished into thin air.

He decided, given the measures they had taken for their own safety, and despite his lack of confidence in the competence of the police, that he would, nonetheless, tell DI Barcley of Larry's 'signature' at the bottom of the note and also of the fact that he was nowhere to be found.

He rang Barcley who seemed to think that the 'signature' implicated Larry somehow and put out an APB to track him down.

Meanwhile, William, concerned at Larry's absence and feeling in his bones that something was not quite right, decided to speak with the Provost.

The Provost was the Oriel Professor of the Interpretation of Divine Scripture, in fact, an Old Testament scholar, and, nearing retirement, had actually stepped up his efforts to ensure that his successor was left with both a clean slate and few problems. He listened at length, with his fingers steepled under his chin in the Provost's study, to William's concerns and then quietly, almost reverently, as was his way, concurred that William was right to speak with him; that no drastic action should be taken until Larry was found; that it would be a good idea for William to contact Larry's parents in the States; that, at the very least, a medical certificate should be required before Larry was allowed to continue his studies. William was grateful to the Provost, in many ways his mentor, and undertook to phone Andy Verity as soon as possible.

As he sat in his drawing room, looking out over Front Quad, he practised his breathing exercises, having taken a good dose of Ventolin, to ameliorate the wheezing the cause of which, he had no doubt, was Larry's peculiar behaviour. And, just as he was working up the courage to phone Larry's father, the phone rang.

'Professor Adams?'

'Yes?'

'It's DI Barcley here. We have some news. Mister Verity, it appears, left England just over a week ago and, according to passport control, appears now to be somewhere in France.

'I've been in contact with Interpol who are looking at their hotel reservation database to see if they can track him down. I'll let you know as soon as we have anything.'

'Why on earth would he go to France? Particularly without telling anyone?'

'Doubtless we'll know the answer to that when we find him.

'I've asked for a court order to gain access to his flat where I hope we'll be able to look at his computer and see if that reveals whether or not he is the author of the notes.'

'I seriously doubt that,' said William.

'Why?'

'He's only been here a short time. I can't imagine he has a motive for wanting to kill me. He can't be that mad...'

'What makes you think that?'

And it was obvious: William had no good reason to think that. Larry's behaviour was very odd indeed; his disappearance strange. If anything, William should suspect the very opposite: Larry might not need a reason to want William dead; he was simply barking mad. He hoped it was not so.

William thanked Barcley for his call and promised to be in contact should there be any further developments from his side. He was now more determined than ever to ring Larry's father.

It took over and hour of repeated attempts but, eventually, he managed to track Andy Verity down. He was alarmed to get such a hostile reception.

'Andy, it's William Adams.'

'Yes, Professor Adams?' This, in itself, was odd: they'd used first names ever since Dom's funeral but now Andy had reverted to a formality that did not portend well.

'I'm ringing because we're worried about Larry.'

'Yes?'

'It seems he's disappeared. I've alerted the police and they have discovered that, without telling anyone, he has gone to France.'

'Yes. In fact, he's in Paris.

'I have to say, Professor Adams, that I think you've driven him there!'

'What?!'

'He tells me that you have been dismissive of his work; that you have been frequently absent. And that you have been rude to him.'

'That's preposterous!'

'There is no need to raise your voice with me, Professor Adams. And I must tell you, I am recording this conversation.'

'What?!'

'You have made no allowances for my son's disability. You have treated him with contempt. I have to tell you that I am considering legal action …'

'You can't be serious… What disability?'

'My son is bipolar and could well do without the bullying sort of behaviour you have subjected him to.'

'Bipolar? Bullying!?'

'Yes. What people like you used to call manic-depression. I think we've said enough. You will be hearing from my lawyers …'

And with that, the line went dead.

William was staggered. He'd had no indication that Larry had any kind of disability. He was unaware that he'd been 'dismissive of his work', such as it was; that he'd been 'bullying'. The idea that it was William who'd 'driven' Larry to France was outlandish.

But at least now things began to make sense: Larry's apparent mood swings, his bizarre essay offerings, his absences and failure to meet deadlines. These might all, from William's dim understanding of the pathology of bipolarism, account for all these strange behaviours.

William alerted both the Provost and DI Barcley to his call with Andy Verity.

CHAPTER 34

They decided on a blade as the instrument of the Prophet's wrath, peace be upon him. A blade was clean. In the right hands it was decisive, final: a head severed from its neck in a single blow ... Well, usually, at least. They would buy a knife, suitable for their purpose, at their destination.

They caught the Oxford bus from Bradford Interchange Bus Station. Their journey would take just over six hours. What they did not know was that two of their fellow passengers – a middle aged, mousey woman engrossed in *Hello* magazine, and an older man, sitting behind the brothers, who never took his eyes off the built-up scenery – were both CTB operatives.

The bus stopped at Derby to take on more passengers and fuel. At which point the two CTB personnel departed but were replaced by a young couple, holding hands, canoodling in the first throes of love, but actually alert to anything they might overhear between Mohammed and Waheed.

The Oxford bus terminal, in Gloucester Green, a market square, was an un-crowded, unhurried place. As they alighted, they asked the driver in which direction they might find 'the colleges'. With a wry smile he pointed them to Beaumont Street and, behind it, St Giles.

'There's plenty of colleges up that way,' he smiled at their touristical backs as they followed his directions.

Beaumont Street offered no shops that sold knives, nor St Giles. They traipsed up Broad Street, past the wall of columns sporting, at their pinnacles, huge heads whose lubricious lips seemed to smack obscenely at the skimpy-topped female tourists about their business in the burgeoning summer weather. No knives.

They felt that asking directions for knives might cause alarm, blow their cover. So they seemed destined to fumble their way around bookshops, tourist emporiums, eateries galore, all useless.

After an hour and a half, their dejection growing, they found themselves outside a huge arcade, announcing itself as Westgate. Even here, it took them a further 15 minutes, on two levels, to find a shop with a kitchen department that sold knives.

It was when they lingered over the large kitchen knives that the CTB staffers who'd been following them from the bus station became concerned about intercepting them.

CTB internet hacking of the brothers' laptops had revealed William Adams and Robin Atwell as their likely targets. Their unusual excursion to Oxford indicated that they were here for a purpose other than tourism. Their loitering over hefty bladed knives meant that their nefarious intentions were, if not imminent, then at least to be enacted soon.

The CTB tail now knew not only that they were singularly unfamiliar with Oxford but that their ramblings could now be understood in the light of the purchase they were about to make: they bought two identical carving knives, Japanese, about nine inches long and two inches wide, tapering to a sharp, narrow point.

Both operatives rang in their reports with both, independently, coming to the same conclusion: having secured their weapons they would now search out their prey.

Mohammed and Waheed left John Lewis, each carrying a paper bag containing their weapon of choice in search of the infidels soon to pay for their crimes. *Inshallah.*

While reluctant to ask directions for knives, they had no compunction seeking the way to Oriel College, the sort of thing any tourist might ask.

Sam Wilson had helpfully revealed that Adams and Atwell were now living together at his College. Wilson, almost daily, provided new photos of his favourite couple, thus making it easy for Mohammed and Waheed to identify their prey. This, of course, was not necessary: Mohammed, in particular, having fantasized about it without ceasing, knew Robin Atwell's face as well as he knew his own.

All they had to do was find the College, wait for them to appear, and dispatch them to Hell.

It was on the seventh request for directions that they finally encountered someone who both new the way to Oriel and was willing to help them.

As they crossed from Carfax into The High, the target was now only 200 yards away, down a side street. They were unaware of the busyness of the airwaves alerting all pertinent players of plans about to be enacted. By sheer happenstance, William and Robin were in his rooms in Oriel. DI Barcley, on instructions from the CTB, phoned to advise them to bolt the door, remain where they were and, within the next two minutes, to admit a plainclothes detective by the name of Gerber. This they duly did as Gerber rebolted the door, moving a chair opposite it, where he took up position, his pistol sitting in his lap, safety off.

Whilst still in John Lewis, the female sergeant following the brothers had been instructed immediately to proceed to Oriel College, there to identify herself to the Duty Porter who had been alerted to her imminent arrival. She had reached the Porters' Lodge a good five minutes before Mohammed and Waheed and now stood behind the glass partition, eyes peeled, pretending to be a porter. Barcley and his sergeant were in their car, also five minutes away.

But a group of ten riot officers, having been called from the local station on the brothers' arrival in Oxford, 'just in case', their van out of sight in the Old Bank parking lot in Magpie Lane, were quietly making their way down the lane into the top end of Merton Street and positioning themselves there, just around the corner from the entrance to Oriel, and out of sight of the suspects coming down from The High.

Mohammed and Waheed's plan was simple, foolproof they thought: go to the College, ask to see Professor William Adams and Dr Robert Atwell, kill them, and, if they managed to inveigle their way into his apartment, they could rape her first.

It was at the Porter's Lodge that pandemonium ensued.

Mohammed, as politely as he had rehearsed, informed the female porter that he and his colleague, Dr al Farabi, had an appointment with Prof William Adams and Dr Robin Atwell.

'Of course,' she said, moving behind the wall towards the door into Front Quad. 'I'll just let you in,' she called over her shoulder as she unholstered her pistol while simultaneously opening the channel on her jacket-buttoned radio: 'They're here,' she spoke quietly and calmly into the mike.

The plainclothes officer in William's rooms jumped to his feet, gun in hand.

The riot police rounded the corner, were momentarily blinded by the fact that the brothers were past the gate, in the alcove outside the Lodge.

The female sergeant had opened the door to the Lodge, stepped into the same space as the brothers, her revolver raised, pointing at them.

'Drop your weapons!' she demanded, evenly, without wavering.

It all seemed to happen so quickly.

Mohammed shouted '*Allahu Akbar.*'

Waheed joined him. Again and again they praised God.

At the same time, Mohammed drew his blade from the paper bag, simultaneously releasing it from its plastic sheath, the price tag sitting in the crook between his forefinger and thumb.

By now the riot police had entered the alcove, fanning around the two, now almost in comic pose.

While still shouting 'Allah is great' at the top of his voice, Waheed was unable to remove the knife from its plastic case. He fumbled with it frantically, eyes full of terror at the multitude of guns turned on him.

It was within a moment that the cunt woman had demanded that they drop their weapons that Mohammed lunged at her, slashing the knife as viciously as he could.

She stepped back a pace. Fired a single round. Mohammed fell to the ground, a slug in his brain.

Waheed, still crying his mantra, had by now released the knife. Seeing his brother lie dead at his feet, he threw himself in the direction of the riot officers, flailing wildly, hoping to inflict maximum damage.

He, too, fell in a volley of bullets, his momentum arrested, along with his life.

When the sergeant posing as a porter announced the all clear, Robin had collapsed into William's arms, sobbing noisily. They'd heard the single shot, followed by many others, all consequent upon the next.

By the time DI Barcley arrived, only minutes later, William had quietly determined that this madness needed to come to an end.

He was mentally calculating the relative safety of Venice *versus* Sydney.

By now his and Robin's faces were so internationally renown that anonymity was impossible.

But the Muslim community of Sydney was hardly supine, often criminal, and certainly given to killing each other.

Another interlude in Venice with its tolerant, well-known friends and acquaintances would be their destination.

Bugger Barcley and his weasel words of assurance.

CHAPTER 35

While he regretted the death of the three kitchen staff, he lost no sleep over his mistake. Indeed, how was he to know that Adams would decide, at the last minute, to cancel his College lunch?

Clearly Adams would be troubled by the deaths meant for him. That the poisoning was contrived for him had been made clear by the ever-helpful Sam Wilson in his running commentary on Adams' life in *Oxford Intrigues*.

Although disconcerted by their unexpected return to England, it did not take long before he learned, from his hacking of Adams' correspondence with his secretary, that another trip to Venice was on the cards.

Given that the pair of them were suffering, he could not miss the opportunity, before they flew the coop again, to intensify their pain: it was time for another note.

He had learned his lesson from his first trip to Venice: this was an operation which required meticulous planning. He could not hope to fumble about aimlessly, the prospect of Adams' death falling serendipitously into his lap.

So plan he did.

At first he thought that it would be simplest to dispatch Adams with a knife. And indeed it would. Knives can be purchased anywhere. But that would also be the riskiest option. Unless he found Adams on one of his solitary excursions, he would have to kill them both. And in Venice, teeming with a quarter of a million visitors a day, his chances of both success in two murders *and* escape were slim.

While passing a weapon through airport security was nigh on impossible, he was assured, from his dark web site, that a pistol, produced by 3D printer, capable of firing four shots, and all made of 'composite material', undetectable by airport scanners, would fit the bill. He bought the gun at huge expense.

He pored over maps of Venice, memorizing street names, routes, landmarks, paying particular attention to the places they had frequented on his first visit: the bar for breakfast, the Rialto markets, the bar at the Guidecca Canal for evening drinks, and, of course, the environs of their apartment. He surprised himself at just how easily he developed a familiarity with the pathways of the city.

And while he conducted his research, he mentally composed his third note. By now, he imagined, they would have cracked his earlier cryptic threat. Now it was time to be even more enigmatic.

And so it was that he printed, using the same typeface as the first two notes:

EARTH! RENDER BACK FROM OUT THY BREAST

A REMNANT OF OUR SPARTAN DEAD!

OF THE THREE HUNDRED GRANT BUT TWO,

TO MAKE A NEW THERMOPYLAE!

He'd donned an anonymous baseball cap and carried the note, sealed in an envelope with PROF WILLIAM ADAMS, ORIEL COLLEGE, typed on the front in the same typeface, into The High on a busy Saturday afternoon. The city centre was packed, principally, he observed, with tourists. Which suited his purposes perfectly.

He'd worn his contact lenses, sun glasses and a dirty grey track suit that he sometimes used for gardening.

On the corner of The High and King Edward Street, stood a group of six, Japanese he assumed, tourists. All appeared to be in their early twenties. He'd not had to wait long before they appeared and decided immediately that they fitted the bill.

He approached the loudly dressed girl with the skirt that revealed far too much of her lumpen legs and asked if she spoke English.

'Yes, I speak English,' she replied.

'How would you like to make £100?'

She eyed him suspiciously. By now, her friends were taking notice in this exchange and this seemed to embolden her.

'Piss off, old man,' she said.

'No. Just hear me out,' he said. 'All I ask is that you deliver this envelope to the porters' desk down at that college,' and here he pointed in the direction of the main gate to Oriel, fifty yards away, 'And once you do, I will give you £100.'

'What this about?' she asked, still wary, but clearly interested in so much cash for so little.

As if reading her mind, he flashed five £20 notes from his top pocket, splayed in his hand.

'It doesn't matter. Look. It's a simple envelope.' He flapped it up and down between his Vaseline-covered fingers. 'All you have to do is take it down to that entrance, hand it to the man behind the desk, come back here, and I will give you the money.

'You can take someone with you if you like and I'll wait here with the rest of your friends. When you get back, I'll give you the £100. What could be easier?'

It was not clear whether it was the perversity of the request, or its novelty that meant she stood there, clearly rehearsing her options.

'Give me letter. I do it.' It was another of her group who offered. She was dumpy, badly dressed and sported a cheeky smile.

'Done,' he said, handing her the letter.

A brief argument ensued as the first girl decided to object to her friend's intervention. 'He ask me, not you …'

But by then the second girl had grabbed the letter and was already on her way down the street towards the College entrance.

He smiled as he watched her go, fat legs pumping, and enjoying the background harrumphing from her disappointed friend.

When the girl returned, her mission complete, he gladly handed over the £100 and quickly melted into the crowds around Carfax.

By the time the police were called in to investigate the note, the Japanese girl and her friends would, he reckoned, be long gone. Besides, porters were passed literally hundreds of notes a day. The prospect of a porter remembering who it was who delivered the note was infinitesimal and, given his disguise, by no way traceable back to him.

CHAPTER 36

William and Robin were due to leave for Venice, using the same subterfuge as before, in two days' time. But William had decided that he would like to complete unfinished business before their departure.

The high table at Oriel College dining room was wide, so conversation across it had to be conducted with voices raised to be heard above the hubbub of the chatter rising to the medieval rafters from the hall.

William thought he detected an uneasiness in Prof Hamish Grant as, after grace was said in Latin, he sat, nodding an awkward greeting in William's direction. The police had interviewed Grant and, having not made clear why he was a suspect in threats to Prof William Adams, had left him in something of a quandary.

It was time, William thought, to confront this particular demon.

'I say, Hamish,' said William over the silverware centrepieces sitting between them across the table, 'I know it's not your field – the law, I mean – but tell me: what are your thoughts on slander and its remedies?'

Affecting a cynicism which his eyes betrayed, Grant responded, 'I'm sure I haven't a clue what you're talking about.'

'Slander, Hamish. You're a linguist. You know the word, I'm sure.'

'Of course, I know the word ... from the Latin, *scandalum* via the Middle English *sclaundre*. It means: to make a false accusation maliciously. But what on earth are you on about?'

Detecting an edge to the conversation, neighbours to both men took an interest in what was transpiring.

William, ignoring the question, ploughed on: 'Quite so. But what is the remedy?'

'I have no idea. I'm not a lawyer. I assume it would be a civil matter. But why are you asking me?'

'Now what, apart from criminal matters, would you say is the most heinous crime of which an academic might be accused?'

'What?!' Grant was starting to lose his composure. The slick façade of world-weary suaveness was slipping away.

'Well, if someone asked me what it was, I'd say plagiarism was the worst crime of which we academics might be accused. Wouldn't you agree? Because, you see, plagiarism strikes at the heart of what we do; it's a lie, and it's theft. And, I think, it poisons the relationship that we have with our students, that commitment we share with them in our joint search for the truth ...'

'I ... well ... I ...'

'And just in which areas of my academic life have I plagiarized the work of others? It can't be the publication of the text of the Cylinder of Babylon: that was a direct translation from the Old Sumerian cylinder. And the same must be said for what they quaintly call the Adams Stela: that was a direct translation from the Middle Egyptian and Meroitic texts on the rock.

'And I can't have plagiarized my work on the *Meroitic Lexicon* because that hasn't even been published yet. So, I wonder what it could be? Which of my books or articles have I plagiarized, I wonder?'

'This is preposterous,' said Grant, throwing his napkin to the ground and making as if to leave.

It was only as he did so that Grant realized that the whole high table had gone quiet; that all eyes were on him. Uneasily, he sat back down.

'Before you leave, Hamish,' said William, unperturbed, 'I think you should know that I have four sworn affidavits, concerning the night of the 22nd, last month. All from witnesses at Christ Church high table dinner that night stating that, to any who would listen, you said, I quote, you "had it on good authority" that I am a plagiarist ...'

Grant squirmed, his eyes firmly on his untouched meal. 'I said no such thing,' he mumbled unconvincingly.

The whole table was now engaged, enthralled.

'And what's more, Hamish, my lawyers, Quilters,' said William, naming one of London's top five legal firms, 'you may have heard of them; they also have copies of those affidavits and, as we speak, are preparing a letter to you, challenging you to establish your calumny in court.'

An eerie silence now sat heavily over the entire dining room.

The quiet was interrupted as Prof Hamish Grant noisily and violently vomited.

◆ ◆ ◆

It was announced, the next week, that Hamish Grant, Professorial Fellow of Oriel College, Oxford, had taken early retirement.

CHAPTER 37

As William passed by the Porter's Lodge in Oriel College after his skirmish with Hamish Grant, the night duty porter passed him a letter. It was embossed with the acronym SENDIST, something he'd not heard of before.

He settled down in his drawing room with a large glass of Lagavulin, wishing that Robin could be there to listen to his tale of the night's events. She had gone back to Univ. to pack in preparation for their departure to Venice.

On opening the letter, he discovered that SENDIST stood for Special Educational Needs Industrial Tribunal. The letter was signed by a woman who described herself as Judge Colquhoun.

The final paragraph read: *In short, you are accused of discriminating against your student because of his disability. A tribunal will be arranged, in due course, and you will be required to answer the charges.*

William was shocked. Although his earlier conversation with Larry's father had indicated that legal action would ensue, he'd not really believed the threat, nor imagined that some engine of state would be brought to bear against him given that he'd done nothing wrong. More so: he'd only been supportive of Larry when he could easily have refused Andy's request to supervise his son.

William put SENDIST into his search engine and discovered

that these were tribunals, established under Prime Minister Gordon Brown, to ensure that innocent, disabled individuals were not discriminated against because of their disability. He found himself wondering why such tribunals were necessary when the courts were an easy and ready option for those so inclined. His own question was answered when he remembered that Brown had expanded the operations of the state in such a way that, although unemployment was thus addressed and the 'family silver' – in this case, The Bank of England gold reserves - had been sold off at knock-down prices, state spending in boom times meant that the public debt rose to unprecedented levels.

And now William was being caught up in Gordon Brown's steamroller, an innocent victim of excessive and unnecessary litigation.

This nonsense evinced in him a determination to get to Venice as quickly as they could. He'd had enough of the whole Verity affair which served only to compound his sorrow at Dom's death and the imagined obligations arising from it.

He would alert Claire to what had happened and ask her to advise his lawyers accordingly. He would tell the Provost of this new development; he would warn Robin of what had transpired when she arrived, later that evening.

He hoped that Sam Wilson's source in the Thames Valley Police would not get hold of this new, juicy bit of information.

CHAPTER 38

The following morning, as he and Robin made their way through the College entrance towards Quod, for breakfast, the duty porter handed him a note marked: PROF WILLIAM ADAMS, ORIEL COLLEGE.

William recognized the typeface.

Taking Robin's hand, he led her back to his rooms, ignoring her protestations and worried demands for an explanation of what had happened.

Once there, he ripped open the note to reveal its contents. They read it together:

EARTH! RENDER BACK FROM OUT THY BREAST

A REMNANT OF OUR SPARTAN DEAD!

OF THE THREE HUNDRED GRANT BUT TWO,

TO MAKE A NEW THERMOPYLAE!

'What on earth!?' William expostulated, not realizing the pun.

'What can it mean?' asked Robin.

William had had enough; he was fed up of being played with by this demented murderer, whoever he was. He was angry at what he saw now amounted to persecution from Larry Verity and his parents. He was about to suggest that they give up, get the plane to Venice that night and try to escape from it all, when better counsel prevailed: they would try to decipher the note;

they would call the police; and they would catch their plane the following night, as planned.

Robin was becoming distressed, so he took her in his arms and cuddled her for a long time.

'We shall do all we can do,' he said, regaining a modicum of composure. 'We shall try to work out what the note means, we shall ring Barcley, and then we shall disappear as planned.'

And then it occurred to him. He'd been so absorbed in the terror of the whole situation: the threats, the deaths, and now the litigation ... that he'd not considered the first, and most obvious thing: Robin's safety.

'No. I have a better plan. It's *me* he's after,' for reasons he could not articulate, he knew it was a *he*, 'not you. Any danger *you* might be in is because of *me*. The earlier notes make that clear. This is all about my cracking Meroitic. You are incidental to his machinations ...'

Robin was about to object, but he hurried on. 'Don't you see? If it's me he wants then the answer is simple: when I disappear, the danger to you goes with me. If I'm away, you'll be left alone, safe.'

'And just how long do you propose to be away so that I can be safe?' she was angry.

'As long as it takes. Till they find him?'

'So you are happy to desert me, to swan off to Venice ... or wherever, and to wait while our bungling Mr Plod eventually manages to track down this maniac!? And you think I'm going to be happy just to get on with my own life without a care in the world while this nutter does his damnedest to track you down? Is that really what you think? And what makes you so sure I'm *not* at risk?'

'I have no intention of letting you wander off on your own.' Clearly, Robin was adamant.

He was overcome by her desire to protect him, to be with him, even though this placed her in mortal danger.

He drew her to him in another embrace, as tears formed in his eyes.

After they had stood there thus for what seemed to them both like an age, cocooned in the safety of each other's arms, she whispered in his ear: 'It's a quote.'

William was lost. It took him some time to realize that she was referring to the note.

'A quote from what?'

'It doesn't matter from what. We need to keep a sense of proportion here. I'm not going to be beaten by this shit.' And with that, she quickly undid her blouse and lifted her bra up and over her breasts.

'What are you doing?'

'Isn't it obvious?' she said as she fumbled at his trouser front.

'Now? Of all times?'

'Absolutely now of all times.' She worked her hand into his boxers and held his responding penis. All William could do was let out a soft moan, as she moved back to the wall, pulling him with her. Her skirt, unbuttoned, fell to the ground, followed by her knickers.

He savoured the kiss and the urgency with which she manoeuvred him inside her as his trousers dropped around his ankles, along with the note.

With one hand cupped around a breast, the other around her buttock, he moved in harmony with her swaying hips, gently thrusting together as their tongues too moved in concert. They came together as both somehow knew they would.

Although it was only breakfast time, William didn't need much persuading that they pondered the latest note over a Bloody Mary. They sat together on the drawing room sofa, Robin playing gently with William's now errant hair as he puzzled at the note.

'I've heard it before,' said Robin. 'I know it's a quote but I just can't place it at the moment. It's obviously poetry from the metre. It'll come to me before too long.'

'There's an easy way to work it out,' said William, rising and moving to the bookcase behind them. From there he extracted a heavy tome, *The Oxford Dictionary of Quotations*. 'It's bound to be in here.' And with that he turned to the back of the book, about to look up "Thermopylae".

'Byron,' said Robing triumphantly, before he could find his reference. 'It's from Lord Byron.'

'Indeed it is,' said William, settling on the correct page. 'It comes from his *Don Juan*, the third canto. Well remembered!' But then he paused. 'But here's the strange thing. The killer's misquoted …'

'Well, he's got form,' Robin offered.

'Look, it says: " Earth! Render back … blah, blah … Of the three hundred grant but three …" not two. Byron's got "three" but his note says "two".

'So why change *three* to *two*?'

'Maybe we just need to put it in context … the Persian Xerxes had amassed a fabulous force to attack Greece; they should have been overwhelmed. Thermopylae was a narrow coastal pass. Leonidas, King of Sparta, moved north from Sparta with a small force of 300 and occupied the pass. Leonidas' men held out magnificently for two days against the best Xerxes could throw at them. It was almost a victory. But the Persians found an ill-guarded mountain track and moved round on Leonidas' rear. The 300 were killed.

'Not much later, the Greeks under Themistocles, prevailed and Xerxes was sent home with his tail between his legs.'

'That's very impressive,' said William.

'It's kind of my area of expertise: classics, that sort of thing,' she said.

'But what's it got to do with changing *three* to *two*?'

'I don't know. Maybe the three refers to the kitchen staff who died, and the two refers to us?'

'But if that's the case, why "grant but two to make a new Thermopylae?". I assume that with the 300 dead, the two making a new Thermopylae are meant to survive? You don't think this means he's saying that he is going to let us live? That he's giving up?'

'Or maybe the two have to fight Thermopylae all over again?'

'Maybe he regrets having killed the wrong people and he wants to stop his campaign or vendetta, or whatever it is? Or maybe it's just a new threat: we'll have the same battle to fight all over again?'

'I hope you're right about him giving up. But I can't feel confident that you are. The note's just too cryptic.'

And then it occurred to him: Byron lived in Venice; he owned a palazzo on the Grand Canal, opposite and not far from William's apartment in Dorsoduro. Knight Frank, the estate agents, recently had it on the market for ten million pounds.

William blenched. Robin noticed: 'What?'

'Byron lived in Venice,' he said. 'You don't suppose he knows we've been there?'

'Impossible,' she said, mustering as much confidence as she could but not quite succeeding. 'I mean … the only people who know we went there are Claire, Rick and, well … Nonna. None of them would disclose anything. Would they?'

'No. I'd trust them all with my life. I'm sure it's just a coincidence.'

'I think we still need to get back to Venice where we'll at least be anonymous and certainly safer than we've been here.'

'I agree. But we should get this to Barcley in case they can get something from it. Maybe fingerprints?' said William.

'That's unlikely. He's not been so clumsy before ...'

'Yes, but nor has he delivered a note via the porters before.'

◆ ◆ ◆

DI Barcley was knocking on the door to William's rooms within half an hour of their phoning Thames Valley Police.

'What on earth's this?' he asked, having read the note and unknowingly repeated William's pun.

'It's a quote from Lord Byron, *Don Juan,* third canto,' said Robin.

'What's this stuff about Thermopyle? I know about the 300. Saw the film. Fantastic.'

'It's Thermopylae,' Robin corrected, 'and our man has changed Byron's quote from *three* to *two.*'

'Can you make any sense of this?' Barcley asked.

Robin was about to tell him of their earlier conversation, when William interrupted: 'No. We can't determine what it means. Of course, as you know, Thermopylae was a blood bath. Maybe that's what he's threatening.'

Robin was aghast but managed to hide her consternation at this strange direction William was taking.

'Right,' said Barcley, clearly non-plussed.

After he'd left with the note and the envelope, William having copied them both, Robin pressed William for an explanation.

'We can't really put ideas in his head when we're not sure ourselves,' he said. 'What if we told him that it might suggest an end to this whole affair? Would that, sub-consciously at least, mean that he eased up on the investigation? He's pretty useless at the best of times, but he's all we've got. Best to keep him on message in the hope that he might by accident stumble across the murderer.'

Robin saw the logic of William's conclusions. 'So what do we do?'

'As we agreed. We go to Venice tomorrow and leave this madness behind us.'

◆ ◆ ◆

'I want a tail put on those two,' said DI Barcley as he walked with his sergeant to their car, parked illegally outside the College gates.

'Yes, Sir. Around the clock?'

'You bet your cotton socks. I wouldn't trust them as far as I could throw them.'

CHAPTER 39

It seemed like an age to Robin, but finally the night of their departure for Venice arrived. They'd packed lightly, having left some clothes and necessities back in the Venice apartment, and were now prepared for their clandestine escape.

It was just on 1.30am.

Rick, William's driver of many years' service, had, as arranged, reconnoitred the environs of the College before he prepared to pick them up. A retired sergeant major in the Royal Engineers, responsible for many years for training squaddies, he was canny, competent, and utterly loyal. He'd parked at the top end of Merton Street, by the Examination Schools and not far from the Warden's Lodge.

He walked down the awkward, cobbled road and, as he reached the junction with King Edward Street, peeked gingerly around the corner to the College entrance and beyond.

He was not surprised, having been alerted to the possibility by William, to see a Ford Mondeo, several years old and much the worse for wear, sitting opposite the College gates on a double yellow line, abutting the back of Christ Church and its glorious Wren library. There were two men in the front seat of the car; one appeared to be asleep, his head against the back rest, his jaw slack. The other had the car's interior light on and seemed to be reading a book.

Rick mentally chided them for their amateurishness.

As he turned back towards the Bentley, he rang William, as previously agreed.

'You've got "friends" sitting outside the College, Sir.'

'OK. Plan B.'

'Yes, Sir. See you in ten minutes.'

William told Robin that they had company, so they both swung into the action dictated by Plan B: they carried their bags quietly through to Third Quad. There they took the tunnel to the King Edward Street site and from there out into the road, heading for The High. The buildings of the King Edward Street site obscured them from the parked police, and from The High they were able easily to make their way down, past All Souls and Queen's, to Longwall.

Rick, in the meantime, had turned the car around in Merton Street, gone the wrong way down the one-way section in front of the Examination Schools, and turned right into The High. His next left was Longwall, abutting Magdalen College's long curtain wall, where he parked, waiting for his passengers.

Two minutes later, they were off in the direction of the A40 and thereafter Hanborough, Bladon and on to Kidlington and Oxford airport, where their jet awaited them.

CHAPTER 40

Nonna was, of course, delighted to have them back in the apartment. She genuinely loved William and clearly was beginning to feel the same way about Robin.

It was a Wednesday and it was remarkable just how easily they had slotted back into the happy routines they had established not that long before. It was equally remarkable that Barcley, in admonishing them earlier for their 'unauthorized' absence, hadn't thought to enquire where they had gone. They felt confident that while their absence would soon be noted, their whereabouts would remain a mystery.

After the night's excitement, they were both famished and decided, against habit and inclination, for a late *prima colazione* at *Impronta*. As they sat at a window table, watching the passers-by, William suggested to Robin that he would like to spend the day, with her, in Cannaregio, in fact in the Ghetto. They'd not been there together before and William thought she would like to see it.

'Besides, it's not far from Tintoretto's house and his church, Madonna dell' Orto, where he is buried, and da Robia, one of Venice's best restaurants.'

'I'd love to,' she said, although she suspected that William had something else on his mind.

They decided that they would go to dell'Orto first so they

alighted the vaporetto at Ca' d'Oro, famous as the most beautiful Gothic palace in Venice, and made their way along the congested Strada Nova then, following a serpentine route leaving Robin thoroughly lost, onto Corte dei Muti and then to the less crowded Fondmenta dei Mori which led to the Campo dei Mori, the Square of the Moors, named after the three Moors which are carved on its walls. One Moor, wearing an oversized turban, and standing at an angle enforced over time by shifting foundations, stood guard by the front door of what was Tintoretto's house.

'He and his family lived here until his death in 1594. As you know, he painted the Scuola San Rocco. But arguably his finest paintings are just around the corner, in his parish church.

'I think he's not in the same mindset as Giorgione, or Titian, or maybe even Giovanni Bellini. Actually, that's not right,' he corrected himself. 'He's just *so* different. There's something visceral in the way he paints. And his palate is ... well, unique. You can spot one of his paintings from a mile away and that can't be said for the others. They used to call him *il furioso* for his phenomenal energy. Come ...' he took her hand, 'let's see.'

As he led her through the campo towards the bridge opposite the imposing Gothic church, Robin marvelled at his sensitivity to the beauty around him. He not only cared deeply for the art about which he knew so much, but somehow it informed his being, acted as a prism through which his world was seen and coloured and probably, most importantly of all, felt. She had never met anyone for whom these pictures transformed and informed his life. And she loved him all the more for it.

It came as something of a surprise that the Madonna dell'Orto, the Lady of the Garden, was almost empty. The church, originally dedicated to St Christopher, was renamed after the fifteenth century discovery of a statue of the Virgin Mary in a nearby vegetable garden.

'The statue is in a side chapel, near Tintoretto's grave; it has miraculous powers,' he said, as they stood admiring the façade and the campanile with its onion-shaped cupola.

'You don't really believe that stuff,' she mocked.

'It's not stuff, I'll have you know,' he smiled. 'The miraculous is the locus where the transcendent touches the mundane. It's where the gods truly speak to us.'

Robin realized he was serious, and wanted to examine his apparent 'faith' further but before she could engage him he took her hand again and led her into the church.

On entering, the first thing she noticed was the wall to her left, stained where a painting had been removed. Closer inspection revealed a small sign noting that here had hung a Bellini, *Madonna and Child*, stolen from the church for the third time in 1993 and never recovered. She felt crestfallen. How could someone do such a thing?

As if reading her mind, he said: 'It was probably stolen to order. Some Mafia boss or other fancied it on the wall in the study of his palazzo.'

'The bastards,' was the best she could offer, given how angry she was.

He led her to the right of the great west door to look at the masterpiece *St John the Baptist and Four other Saints* by Cima da Conegliano, who worked mostly in Venice at a time a little earlier than Tintoretto. They had hardly set foot in the church and already she was beginning to be overwhelmed: the interior was faced almost entirely in brick but somehow managed to be light, uncluttered, almost ethereal. William's 'transcendent touching the mundane' was blossoming in her heart.

Having dipped his fingers in the stoup of holy water by the entrance door, he now genuflected as he led her into the central nave aisle, looking up to the red glowing light of the presence hanging above the high altar. As they moved through the nave, she was vaguely aware of more pictures in the transepts; Tintorettos, she was sure. They approached the chancel, and the towering painting on the right loomed ever more dauntingly over her.

'It's *The Last Judgement*, painted by the great man himself.'

She knew he meant Tintoretto. Bodies writhed, swept this way and that from torrents emerging miraculously from nowhere. At one point she thought she saw Charon, the boatman, ferrying the souls of the dead across the black River Styx. The agony of the dead was palpable. She had to look away.

But in averting her eyes, she was confronted, on the left wall, by *The Adoration of the Golden Calf*, the very like of which, the idolatry, had led to the judgement opposite. It was beginning to get to be too much.

And as if to lighten the mood, he said: 'Look at the figure carrying the calf, fourth from the left. It's said that that's Tintoretto himself.

'It always strikes me that, by putting himself in the place of a principal worshipper of the calf he is making his confession. It's a *mea culpa* for his sins in the hope of avoiding the fate of those he painted opposite.'

He clearly detected the emotion brewing inside her. So he took her to the small chapel to the right of the chancel and there, set in the floor, was the grave.

Robin noticed immediately that his name was written: *Jacopo Robusti, Tinctoretto*.

'So you see, it was not Tintoretto: the little dyer. Named after his father's profession. It was Tinctoretto: the little colourist,' said William, as if reading her mind. 'They say that, in an inscription over his studio, he had written *Il disegno di Michelangelo e d'il coloreto di Tiziano*, Michaelangelo's drawing and Titian's colouring. What an ambition!'

It occurred to Robin that William was stage-managing their tour of the church, building up to a climax; first, the empty wall with the missing Bellini, then the Conegliano, then the even more majestic Tintorettos. Now his grave. What could possibly follow?

The answer to her unspoken question came within seconds as he took her to the nearby Chapel of San Mauro where stood the restored statue of the Madonna, for whom the church was now named.

A chill ran through her as the numinous quality of the Madonna's presence spoke to her. She could feel herself being overcome by something beyond her. Maybe the gods *were* speaking to her?

'A *mysterium tremendum et fascinans*,' he said, breaking the spell which held her. But now she was coming to understand what he'd meant earlier by the transcendent meeting the mundane. And it truly was miraculous.

'Shall we eat?' he asked, taking both her hands in his and kissing her gently on the lips as the Virgin looked on, smiling her benediction. But even then the spell was not broken.

They crossed the bridge again and found da Robia by the statue of the same name. By the restaurant, on a corner, stands the figure of Signor Antonio Robia, apparently a figure of malicious fun and satire, his Jewish nose had been rubbed away by centuries of jokers, only to be replaced with a metal one in the nineteenth century.

She was glad of the break that eating their meal provided. The church, the magical Madonna, and the heartbreaking paintings, together with William's talk of things unearthly, was becoming too much to bear.

They ate *Calamaretti e Seppioline alla griglia* to start, with a bottle of dry, crisp, steely Friuli from the Veneto. For mains, he had *Coniglio con Carciofi* and she the *Fegato alla Veneziana*. Given the heavy sauce with both meals, William decided on a light red, a Rondinella from Corvina, also from the Veneto.

It was during this feast that William confessed that he felt the need to go to the Ghetto to, as he put it, 'put things in perspective'. William was not much given to talking about his feelings; not one who could be accused, as he would see it, of introspection. You just got on with life and responded as best, and as honestly, as you could to the vagaries that fortune and happenstance threw at you. It was a simple, undemanding philosophy. But he had been under strain of late, as he knew had Robin.

Having paid the bill, and farewelled the owner, an attractive middle-aged woman who appeared to Robin to be far too familiar with William, they made their way to the Cannaregio Canal which traverses a distinctive part of the city. A sottoportico diverged right from the fondamenta into the Ghetto.

'It comes from "*getto*",' he said. 'This area, effectively an island within Venice, was once a foundry. Getto means "to cast" metals. This, my gorgeous girl, is the world's original ghetto.'

And with that, they passed into a large, open square. The first thing Robin noticed was the guard-post, manned by armed carabiniere. The second was that the buildings around the campo were so much taller than elsewhere in the city, most being seven or eight storeys high.

'In 1516, Jews were confined to living in this part of the city,' said William. 'They could move about the town freely during the day time but they had to be here after curfew for the night. The quarter is cut off by wide canals and two water-gates – the only ways in – and the authorities had these manned by Christian guards who ensured that no Jews were allowed out.

'The Council of Ten even had the effrontery to charge the Jews for the cost of the sentries. Just imagine, paying for the privilege of being imprisoned! Because they couldn't live elsewhere in the city they had no option, as their numbers grew, but to build upwards!

'When they moved about the town they had to wear badges and

caps to identify them. Sound familiar? And they could only trade in textiles, medicine and, of course, money-lending. They were confined to this quarter until 1866. But even now, some choose to live here.'

'Why are there guards here?' asked Robin.

'Yes, it's alarming isn't it. They've been here since 2002. The Venice authorities got a tip-off from the police in Milan who had arrested eight al Qaeda terrorists and discovered that, among other targets, they intended to blow this place up.

'There are five synagogues, a museum, a holocaust memorial,' he said, pointing at the long sculpted memorial wall behind the police kiosk, 'Jewish shops, a kosher restaurant, a bakery. And, of course, lots of these flats are occupied by Jews. It would have been quite a coup for the terrorists.

'Then there were the copycat threats, the offensive graffiti, the minor damage, the general anti-Semitism. So the police thought it better to keep a presence here to protect the residents. But sadly it's an inadvertent reminder of the constant threat Jews live under.'

'I'm afraid it's not helped by Israel's current attacks on Gaza,' said Robin.

'Quite. But not really Israel. More Netanyahu and his right-wing cronies. Although, I suspect that the Gaza massacre is something of a side-show …'

Robin registered his comment and determined to follow up on it, but before she could …

'Even so …' They were both overcome by sadness, not just at the appalling treatment of Jews as evidenced by the Ghetto, but of the sufferings of the Palestinian people.

William confessed that the real reason he'd wanted to come here was to put their 'little local difficulties' – the deaths, the threats, the litigation, the publicity, the lack of anonymity – into perspective. He'd hoped that in confronting the reality of suffering on a scale unimaginable that it might make their own troubles seem less oppressive.

'But all I've managed to do is point up what a miserable place the world is!'

'I don't think I could bear to live with a maudlin man,' she protested gently.

'Oh, don't mind me. I'm not given to self-pity.'

And it was true. He wasn't. What he didn't tell Robin was that

today, 12th June, was the seventeenth anniversary of his father's death. It was a day he always found hard to bear. William's mother had died when he was a toddler; he remembered nothing about her apart from the loving memories conjured up by his father of the wife he adored.

But Sir James Adams had died when William was twenty-one. It was the greatest wrench in his life up until the death of his wife Gill and their daughter, Jeny. And, inevitably, all that loss came flooding back, eating away at his eviscerated soul.

Until … Robin had come back into his life. He thanked the gods for the joy that she had brought.

And with that, he took her hand and they walked to a wall with five tall, arched windows. Above them, they could just make out a modest domed skylight indicating the apse of one of the square's synagogues. Between two of the windows, embedded in the wall, was an inscription, written in Hebrew. He read it to her:

'$R^ab^im\ mak^ia^ob^im\ larasha$' $w^eh^abozt^iah\ b^ih^{ye}h\ h^is^ed\ y^em^ib^ib^in^u$. Many are the sorrows of the wicked, but he who trusts in the Lord, loving kindness shall surround him. I think it comes from Psalm 32.'

And with that, and without a word further, he walked her home along the alleyways and streets, foregoing vaporetti, and enjoying instead the bustle and squeeze that was a tourist-filled, thriving Venice.

It was the following day that, for the first time in her life, Robin started a diary.

CHAPTER 41

Claire knew not to ring William in Venice unless it was absolutely necessary. She therefore did so with great reluctance.

It appeared that the Provost of Oriel College had, on William's behalf, been assiduous in following up all lines of investigation into the SENDIST trial.

The application form for entry to Oxford University, question 37, said: 'Do you have any Special Educational Needs or disabilities?' To which the answer, given on Larry's application and in handwriting, was 'No'.

Knowing full well that their child was bipolar, Andy and Kathleen Verity had lied on the University application form thus putting both William, and the Provost, at a severe disadvantage.

Moreover, Claire had researched, in typical fashion, the pathology of someone who was bipolar and had written to William to suggest that Larry's behaviour was typical of someone, with bipolar, who had ceased to take their medication. If they took the pills, then the erratic behaviour, exhibited by Larry, was uncommon. Equally, because of various side-effects, those on medication for manic depression, often did not take their pills thus exacerbating the condition, often leading to suicide.

William knew better than to feel sorry for himself.

He also remembered that Dom Taylor, Larry's uncle and Director of the British Museum team of archaeologists in Babylon, was also bipolar. Under the pressure placed on him by an addition to the team of four unco-operative American scholars, Dom had stopped taking his medication and this had led to his suicide. William vaguely remembered having read somewhere that bipolarism was hereditary, particularly in the male line.

Claire advised him that a university investigation continued and tried to offer assurances that William had nothing to fear. Of course, these blandishments only served to increase the strain that both William and Robin felt.

Both wished that Claire had not sought to remind them of worries back home.

CHAPTER 42

Thursday, 13th June

Walked to Zattere (stopped at S. Trovaso on the way - usually closed – marvelled at the Tintorettos, particularly the large Ultima Cena, hidden away) for vaporetto to Guidecca. Strolled down to Molina Stucky then back to Redentore (Palladio): saw a wedding in progress so didn't go in. The bride was beautiful. No. Really.

On to Zitelle for vaporetto to S. Giorgio Maggiore (also Palladio) – a jewel. More Tintorettos, father and son. A glorious 15thC wood-carved quire. Guidecca quiet, unhurried, unsophisticated.

Home for lunch. I cooked risotto. Quiet afternoon. William drew our street sign; I read.

Early dinner. William cooked fried veal + salad. Then romantic stroll to Danieli to book dinner for next week.

Friday, 14th June

Caught the train from S. L. to Padua at 8.50am. Booted out of our seats at Mestre (didn't realize allocated seating!). The trip was only 20 mins. But got the slow train back – twice the time.

Went straight to the Scrovegni Chapel (Giotto frescoes). Completely overwhelmed.

The Eremitani Church was also magnificent, sadly Mantegna frescoes were destroyed by a bombing raid in 1944 but beautifully restored, a small miracle.

Walked to the centre, saw Pedrocchi Café and arrived at the Duomo just as it was closing. Visited the baptistry – completely covered in

C14th frescoes. Had good lunch overlooking Duomo and Baptistry. William did a sketch of the latter.

Walked to Basilica di S. Antonio, markets, Prato dell Valle (moated garden) & S. Giustina.

Train home at 6.00pm. Takeaway pizza from Campo Margherita for dinner, Early night.

Saturday, 15th June

After Padua yesterday, something of a rest day. Delicious time in bed. A.m. food shopping. Lunch tuna salad. W. drew in pm (detail of Ca' Rezzonico) and I shopped (trousers for me and presents for friends). Evening drinks at Zattere then home for Spag. Bol. W. cooked.

Sunday, 16th June

Lie in then to St. George's (the English church of Venice – you see: he's got me going to church!) for BCP eucharist. Priest (camp, high) liked the sound of his own voice. The gods not present. After service, they shared where the visitors were from ('Hi, I'm Dierdre from Delaware'; 'I'm Ian from Iowa' – oh dear). We kept our counsel in Browning and Ruskin's church. W. suggests we worship in the Frari or S. Marco in future.

Lunch at home then to La Fenice for Rigoletto (who was the star of the show); such a depressing story but a glorious performance. W. precariously jumped (at a great height) into the vacant box next door for a front seat.

Dinner at what was once W.'s favourite Venetian restaurant (Canonica) off S. Marco – food was ok but sadly now turistica.

Lovely walk home in the balmy evening. With W., often feel like a teenage girl in love for the first time!

CHAPTER 43

He splashed out an extra £100 to get an earlier flight on the Friday evening so that, unlike last time, he wouldn't be traipsing into his Air B&B after midnight. If everything went to plan, then he should be able to complete his revenge the following weekend.

He reconnoitred the area about their apartment at seven the next morning and waited till they emerged at ten. In the interim, he allowed himself a quick foray in Campo Barnaba for a takeaway coffee but otherwise remained vigilant and out-of-sight.

They started the day, as he assumed they always did, with coffee and brioche at *Impronta* and then made their way in a leisurely fashion – it was always leisurely; he was becoming irrationally angrier at the ease with which it appeared they conducted their lives – to a market in Campo Santa Margherita, stopping on their way at a barge, moored by Ponte Pugni, to purchase vegetables. This was a change to their normal pattern, he thought. He'd imagined that they always shopped for food at the Rialto. But if they'd risen late, then going to the nearby campo rather than three times that distance to Rialto made sense. As he didn't know what they had done the evening before, he had no means of guessing whether 10.00 was a late rise, accounting for a changed shopping pattern, or whether this was, in fact, their usual time to emerge. There was, he realized, so much about their lives here of which he was ignorant. But he remained convinced that here was a safer place for an assassination: crossed jurisdictions; the notorious incompetence of the Italian police, exacerbated by inter-factional police rivalries; the sheer volume of people in Venice and, of course, his alibi.

He'd travelled on a false passport, purchased from the dark web. He would buy a ticket for a movie at Cineworld, to place him in the Oxford environs on the day he chose to attack. And while it was true that CCTV would be able to identify him at both Gatwick and Marco Polo, he'd been careful to wear sunglasses, a baseball cap and keep his head down at all times. Anyway, why would the police bother to spend the time scrolling pointlessly through airport CCTV?

Their brief shopping excursion completed, they returned to their apartment, presumably for lunch. It annoyed him further that while they spent their carefree time eating and drinking, he had to stand around in the campo, hungry and dependent on their whims for his information. He decided that another brief dash into the bar opposite to buy a sandwich and a drink would not be too great a risk.

At just after 2.00pm, they both emerged, looking oh so smug and pleased with themselves. Then they went in opposite directions: she to the north, possibly towards the Rialto, he back down Calle de le Botthege, towards the Grand Canal.

It was clear to him whom he should follow, but worried that he would be far more visible in the narrow alleyway leading to the vaporetto stop at Ca' Rezzonico.

The woman was quickly lost in the tourist throng heading across Campo Barnaba as Adams made his way down Calle del Traghetto towards the palazzo.

He almost panicked when Adams turned left into a walled garden behind the palazzo, sat on a stone bench and opened his moleskin book, clearly preparing to sketch.

His position was precarious. He could not stand for God knows how long, peeping around a corner, while the shit sat in the sun doodling at his leisure.

He reasoned that, as the only way out for Adams was to catch a vaporetto or return back down Calle del Traghetto, he could position himself in the café opposite the entrance to the calle from which it was likely that Adams must emerge. The danger here would be if the woman returned. But they'd never met, so he felt safe on that account that she couldn't recognize him.

He sat in a window seat at the café, eyes peeled, pretending to read a book, and stringing out the consumption of too many pastries and coffees until he felt ready to burst. He enjoyed watching the people out on *passaggio*. He particularly enjoyed seeing the young Italian men – it was obvious who were the natives – with their tight shorts and trousers, their bare arms and swarthy complexions. Many of them were quite beautiful. At times he had to admonish himself: he was here on serious business. Distraction, no matter how lovely, could not be tolerated. But it was an effort ...

At 6.00pm, she returned carrying shopping bags. She made her way straight for the Calle del Traghetto. It was obvious that she knew where to find him.

And soon they appeared, he carrying the shopping bags – how sickeningly gallant of him – and they arm-in-arm; they were making their way to the apartment.

He was pleased not to have to wait too long before they re-emerged from the apartment and made their way along Cerchieri Toletta towards Fondamenta Sangiatofetti. It was clear to him that they were heading to the Zattere; they had done this last time.

A plan began to form in his mind: if they went to the Zattere again the following night, to the same bar as before, it would be reasonable to assume that they took their aperitifs there each evening. He could reconnoitre the area and, given that they took up their position in roughly the same spot each night, he could determine the place from which he could shoot Adams before slipping away quietly, his exit route already planned. All things being equal, he would execute his plan, and the man who had ruined his life's ambition, the following Saturday night.

He was gratified when they did, in fact, go to the same bar as last time, *Chez Nico*, and purchase what clearly were the same drinks as last time, and occupy roughly the same space by the waterside as last time. Now his planning could begin in earnest.

CHAPTER 44

DI Barcley was furious. Despite his demand that they not leave the city, it was quite clear that they had absconded again.

He had arrived at Oriel to give them the good news of a 'breakthrough' in the case: a partial finger print had been lifted by forensics from the Vaseline-coated corner of the envelope which held the last of the notes. And while it was the Vaseline which had captured the imprint, it was the same substance which had adulterated the sample, making it impossible to retrieve any DNA. Nor had they been able to match the partial fingerprint with any database, including that of Interpol.

In short, they had nothing. But Barcley was grasping at straws and hoped that the partial print might at least be a point of reference for the future.

Having been rude to the porter who advised him of William and Robin's absence for the last five days at least, he fumed in the squad car as he was driven back to the station by his sergeant, who knew better than to break the silence while his DI was in this kind of fug. He was livid that the tail he'd set had obviously failed and, more particularly, had not advised him. He would raise hell when he next saw them.

In truth, Barcley was angry with himself: he knew he should have extracted their whereabouts from them last time, but he had simply overlooked it. And although he chided himself for his oversight, he was secretly in sympathy with their decision to leave: the police could not provide 24-hour protection and, he had to admit, he had no idea who might want to kill this most famous of academics. Although the smart money was on some terrorist group or other, still seething, years after the event, at Adams' temerity in questioning the Prophet's words in the historical parts of the Qu'ran. A *fatwa* was, after all, still live.

◆ ◆ ◆

In spite of the fact that Larry Verity had returned to his apartment in the Woodstock Road, the lack of coordination between the Metropolitan Police and Thames Valley Police meant that Barcley had not been informed.

A telephone call from a concerned Andy Verity, via the SENDIST judge, to the Thames Valley Police, led to their dispatch to his flat in the Woodstock Road where, upon forcing entry, they discovered his body hanging from a rope tied over the top of a door and anchored to the handle behind; his feet dangling barely two inches above the ground. Larry had died three days before he was discovered.

Larry had stopped taking his medication and had chosen the same method of death as his uncle.

Claire, on learning of Larry's death from DI Barcley, decided not to tell William until his return from Venice, whenever that might be.

CHAPTER 45

Monday, 17th June

Early rise, very hot day.

Vaporetto from Ca' Rezzonico to Lido. At S. Maria Giglio stop held up by several police launches to see Mario Monti (former Italian PM, now European Commissioner – we think!) and others escorted onto launches.

Walked the (almost) empty beach and swam.

Film festival & celebrity spotting. W. swears he saw George Clooney as we had drinks at the Hôtel des Bains.

Risotto lunch and vaporetto home.

W. cooked dinner: Filetti di San Pietro con funghi. He likes cooking Enrica Rocca style: fresh, simple, and lots of (too much!) salt.

Tuesday, 18th June

Impronta breakfast. Walk to Zattere via Angelo Raffaele – looking for Miss Garnet's angel (both now reading the book to refresh memory). Found her apartment.

On to Gia Schiavi (Brunetti's favourite bar) for wine and cichetti lunch – the best in town.

Pm. W. to sketch at Archivio di Stato (by the Frari): three ledgers of different lions! W. clearly in his 'lion period'!

Drinks at Nico's then W. made delicious carpaccio, with bottle of Barolo.

Wednesday, 19th June

Up early for 10.27 to Castelfranco. Got there early so visited S. Geremia (saw the remains of S. Lucia – the Venetians specialized in stealing other people's saints). Arrived 11.30 (Italian trains clean, efficient, a pleasant experience – why can't we do this back home?). Went to Giorgione's house.

Great lunch (three course – am eating too much – will get fat, but strange thing is, in spite of all the pasta am not putting on weight) by the Duomo followed by frustrated attempt to get into what looked like a public park.

3.00pm Into Duomo and saw Giorgione's glorious altar piece (for Matteo) – couldn't drag W. away from it.

Home at 4.51 treno alta frequentazione – a joy – then vap. to Ca' Rezzonico.

I cooked. Risotto as usual – he never complains!

Thursday, 20th June

Late start to day. Walk to Scuola Carmini and S. Nicolo dei Mendicoli, the latter closed so revisited pm.

Shopping and cichetti for lunch.

Pm. To Mendicoli (centre of fund-raising for flood defences). W. drew, I read. Rain stopped W.'s drawing.

Trip to Santa Margherita for fish dinner.

Friday, 21st June

Weather changed dramatically – 19 degrees and overcast. Off to Accademia (undergoing extensive refurbishment) so W. misses his favourite Bassanos and Carpaccio BUT Titian exhibition on + 3 Giorgiones! It's magnificent, as is the whole collection. Bought book on Giorgione.

Lunch at home – salads, prosciutto, fresh bread.

Pm. To Palazzo Grimani – glorious, including one of the Giorgione Tedeschi frescoes: La Nuda.

Walk home via Formosa. W. sketches detail from Ca' Rezzonico.

Drinks at Nico's.

W. cooks dinner: Maiale in Tecia. The pork is <u>so</u> succulent. He really is a v. good cook.

I could live this way forever.

CHAPTER 46

He'd arrived the night before and had determined that today would be the day. Although Saturdays seemed to be even more brim-filled with tourists – as if that were possible – that could make the whole exercise that much cleaner: more cover, greater confusion, denser crowds to make following him nigh on impossible.

There was no need to pursue them the whole day: his plan was to attack at evening drinks on the Zattere, at *Chez Nico's*.

As he'd hoped, his composite gun went through customs undetected and the examination of his forged passport, at the height of the tourist season, was cursory at best.

He'd slept in and only arrived at Campo Barnaba for surveillance – just to make sure nothing unusual was happening – at 9.30. Just before ten, they appeared at the small bridge leading to the campo and made their way, as usual, to *Impronta*.

He felt sufficiently confident, at this point, to return to his accommodation. There he checked and loaded the four bullets into the gun, following the instructions with meticulous care. He could not afford for anything to go wrong. He'd never shot a pistol before but had, in the Combined Cadet Force at school, been handy with a 22. Rifle. He would be near enough for it to be virtually impossible for him to miss.

His only luggage was his rucksack.

His plan was simple: follow them to the Zattere for their evening drinks. They were clearly creatures of habit so they would stand, as they always did, on the quayside, right by the water watching the boats go by. While they did so, he would slip into *Nico's*, buy a drink and some crisps, place them on a table and his rucksack on a chair, so that it looked as if someone was sitting there but had simply popped to the toilet, soon to return.

The gun he'd tucked into his waistband, concealed by his jacket. His fake passport, plane ticket, and wallet, he had in his breast pocket, as usual.

Immediately behind where they usually stood were ten or so tables where *Nico's* customers sat. Behind that there was the thoroughfare, about five metres wide, where those enjoying *passaggio* would stroll to and fro; then behind that, more tables leading up to the front of the bar itself.

He would need to position himself on the waterside of the thoroughfare to get a clear shot. The danger here was that they might see him or that customers might be milling about around the tables by the quayside. In which case, he would simply have to play it by ear. If they turned and saw him, he would have to kill them both. If not, it would just be Adams.

They always stood facing the canal, watching the water traffic. Ideally, he could strike when a passenger liner passed, as usually they did at this time of the evening. Always accompanied by two tugs and occupying the main part of the Guidecca Canal, forcing all before them to the side, they were quite a spectacle and, it seemed, their skipper could never resist a farewell blast to Venice's inhabitants on the ship's horn before it entered the Bacino. All in all, the display would provide excellent cover for his operation: the sight to distract anyone from taking much notice of what he was doing, and the horn blast to cover the sound of what he hoped would be a single discharge.

If his shot was clean, and Adams fell immediately, he would make his retreat as planned. If not, he would empty the chamber of all four bullets to make sure of the job. Of course, there were serious risks. But life was full of uncertainty. And although it was a cliché, he firmly believed that *Audaces Fortuna juvat timidosque repellit*. Fortune favours the bold ... and repels the timid. No-one could accuse him of being timid.

He would retreat to the bar, collect his rucksack and head for the bus stop at Piazzale Roma – a fifteen-minute walk depending on crowds, and there catch the No. 5 to the airport. On the way, when it seemed least obvious, he would throw the pistol into any of the dozens of canals he would skirt.

He felt sufficiently confident in his plan that he decided to take himself on an extensive walk of the city, maybe he would even enjoy a slap-up lunch at one of Venice's better class restaurants. He was beginning to enjoy himself.

CHAPTER 47

They had a fabulous day, as it seemed they always did in Venice: nothing palled, nothing became tired or overly familiar, they took nothing for granted.

They'd risen at the usual time and, after *cappuccini e brioche con crema* at *Impronta*, they went to Rialto for that day's food.

On their return they walked down Calle Lunga towards S. Sebastiano, full of Veronese's paintings and frescoes. The sacristy was a mish-mash of artists but was overwhelming still. It was, they decided, a truly beautiful church, boasting a fine gallery.

After lunch, they headed for the Scuola Grande San Giovanni Evangelista, a wealthy scuola with sumptuous interiors full of largely second division artists, Domenico Tiepolo among them. The great joy of their visit was the extraordinary cycle of Palma apocalyptic works in the Sala d'Albergo.

They chortled that the scuola has, since the fifteenth century, been custodian of two slithers of the true cross.

Afterwards, they went, via the Rialto, to La Fenice where they bought tickets for that Sunday's concert and discovered that, in so doing, they became Associates of the *Associazione Culturale Musica Venezia*.

'I never dreamed I'd become an associate of anything to do with music!' Robin joked. She claimed not even to be able to sing in tune.

On their way home, in the row of jewellery shops behind the Rialto, William bought Robin a sapphire bracelet. Robin cried with joy and, there and then, kissed him passionately, much to the embarrassment of the shopkeeper.

She could not wait to get home and write up her diary for the day but she always took time to do this so she succumbed to William's blandishments that it was time for them to go to *Chez Nico* for their aperitifs.

On reaching the Zattere they parted, as always they did, she to secure a place by the water-side with unobstructed views, and he to the bar to buy their drinks: as always, one Campari and one Aperol spritz. He balanced the tray with their crisps, drinks and olives through the ambling crowds to join Robin in their favoured place by the canal.

They'd both come to adore this habitual interlude in their daily round. They'd even developed a silly game, of which they never grew tired: most evenings, at this time, hulking great cruise liners dragged by straining tugs would lumpenly labour their way down the Guidecca, through the Bacino, into the Laguna and then to the sea. Invariably, they would sound their monstrous horns, as if purposely to annoy the locals.

Opposite *Nico's*, and a little to the right on Guidecca, was S. Eufemia, a run-down little church that they had visited early on in their stay in Venice. It boasted an altar piece of S. Roch and an Angel by Vivarini, a painter whose faces were always, they agreed, squashed, making them look like the inbred Appalachians of the film *Deliverance*.

Their game was based on a simple device: they tossed a coin, one choosing heads or tails one day, the other the next (because they threw a euro, it was either Ns, numbers, or Bs, bodies or buildings). The winner got to choose whether the cruise ship would blast its horn before the ship had reached S. Eufemia, or after its prow had passed it. If William won they would have two drinks at *Nico's*, if Robin, then one. It was all very childish, but it was light-hearted fun. The waiters, and particularly Raffaello, with whom they'd become friends, were aware of the game: every time William returned for the second round they knew he'd won. In fact, they were keeping a running total with a small wager of their own on the outcome by the time William and Robin returned to England.

William had now joined Robin at the quayside where he placed the tray, only a little precariously, as usually he did, on top of the wooden flat-topped docking post abutting the quay.

Before they took their drinks, William produced a coin and tossed it in the air.

'Numbers,' said Robin. And numbers it was. William feigned disappointment.

'It's better for your liver,' she said. He kissed her on the cheek. 'And I'll say: before,' as she looked down the Canal and saw the huge hull making its way from Tronchetto towards them. 'Anyway, I haven't won yet ...'

◆ ◆ ◆

He'd followed them from San Barnaba all the way down Fondamenta Sangiatoffetti without being seen. Why should they look back? And if they did, the crowds were sufficiently dense on balmy evenings such as this to mask his presence thirty yards behind. He was confident he was safely concealed.

He lingered at the juncture of the fondamenta with the Zattere while Adams collected their drinks and wended his way through the throng to stand beside the woman. They were clearly both absorbed in their own little world, as always Adams had been, so his path was clear.

As planned, he went into the bar and there found himself one of the many vacant tables; most people preferred to be outside on evenings such as this, especially when the ships passed by. He deposited his rucksack on one of the two chairs, tipped the other up against the rim of the table, just in case, and went to the bar to place his order. It did not take long before an over-friendly waiter served him his beer and the obligatory metal tray of crisps.

Seeing that they were facing away from him, looking, as they had done when he'd observed them before, towards the canal, he ventured out to the path in front of the bar and walked twenty or so paces to the left, the better to get a view down the canal in the direction from which the cruise ships came.

He was in luck. One giant of a ship was making its unstately way up the canal towards him. *Fortune favours the bold ...*

Now was clearly the time, but it was also the moment of greatest risk. As the boat edged its way slowly in their direction, he waited on the bar-side of the thoroughfare, masked from view. He would not cross to the other side until it was time to shoot. Indeed, he had no idea how loud the gun's blast would be. He hoped that the ship's horn would coincide with his firing but could not afford to wait for that to happen.

At one hundred yards distant, the boat would soon be upon them and as he pushed through the crowd, now slowing to get a better glimpse of the passing spectacle, he found himself directly behind the two of them with an unobstructed view.

He removed the gun from his waistband. He knew he couldn't possibly stand in the brace position he'd seen on television – that would draw undue attention – so he held the pistol to his chest, aiming it at Adams' back, now only twelve feet away.

The blast of the ship's horn startled him but equally spurred him into action.

Just as he squeezed the trigger, he was nudged by one of the throng of passers-by, watching the ship, not looking where she was going.

The gun went off, its noise muffled by the ship's horn.

And with a convulsive jolt, Robin Atwell's body was hurled forward, into the water.

CHAPTER 48

Panic set in. He'd killed the wrong person.

And now the crowd, which had stopped to watch the cruise ship pass, surged forward to see the woman in the water. He was being pushed towards the very scene he had brought about.

In an attempt to get a grip on events of which he was quickly losing control, he holstered the pistol in his waistband, turned, and angrily pushed his way through the surge of bodies eager to rubber-neck at the tragedy unfolding before them.

It took what seemed like minutes, but must have been only seconds, to reach the entrance to the bar. He rushed to the table, where his beer and crisps sat untouched, to collect his rucksack. It was gone. He'd left it on the chair. The chair was empty. He searched the immediate area around the table, conscious that every second he spent here increased the chance that he would be caught.

Someone might have seen him shoot! Why had he not shot Adams when he had the chance? He had fucked up monumentally! Even now they might be scouring the crowd looking for him! Or alerting the police!

He could not afford to waste any more time looking for his fucking rucksack. He must leave, he told himself, and do it immediately. He had his passport and wallet and ticket on him.

There was nothing important in the bag. Nothing that could incriminate him.

Or was there?

He left the bar as quickly as he could, without drawing attention to himself. He turned right into Fondamenta Sangiatoffetti heading towards Piazzale Roma and the bus for Marco Polo airport, turning over in his mind the contents of his bag.

Doubtless someone had stolen it. But did it contain anything that might connect it with him? None of his clothes were named. Nor his toiletries. Was there anything else? His book. He was reading a novel. *The Man-Eater of Malgudi* by R.K. Narayan. Had he signed the inside cover, as he did as a matter of course with all his books? He couldn't remember. His panic rose. He was surprised to find that he had reached Campo Carmini, almost half-way there.

What would a thief care about the contents of a stolen rucksack? Nothing much. There was certainly nothing of value in it: underwear, shirts, trousers, toiletries, socks … and the book! Fuck, fuck and double fuck!

But what if it was not a thief? What if the smarmy barman had put it behind the bar for safe-keeping? Then he was sure to be exposed. In an attempt to locate its owner, they would search the contents, find the book … *Did it have his name in it?*

Murder carried a mandatory life sentence. If they found him, he would doubtless be extradited to England. They would discover he'd killed the three college staff. That it was a mistake didn't matter.

His mind was a whirl of questions, implications, possibilities. He wasn't thinking rationally. He needed to calm down, breathe steadily, and take stock.

But now he found he was there. He was crossing the small park that bordered Piazzale Roma and there, as *fortune favoured the brave*, sat a No.5 bus, its engine running and its door open.

He paid the driver and took a seat near the bendy-bit in the middle just as the bus took off, turning its wide circle to head back north, towards the Ponte della Liberta and the airport.

It was only as he started to relax a little, collect his thoughts and quietly consider the enormity of his blunder, that he realized that the pistol was still tucked under his belt.

What more could go wrong? He couldn't even contemplate taking the thing back home. He would need to dispose of it somewhere between the bus and the airport. Obviously, he couldn't just leave it on the bus. It would be discovered in short order and doubtless linked to the murder he'd just committed. The No.5 stop was immediately opposite the departures hall, a mere twenty yards or so. There were bins in the airport. But what if he was seen? There were always armed police aplenty in Italian airports.

His panic returned, along with the bile rising in his throat. With his luck, he would be sick and draw further attention to himself.

Twenty minutes later, as the bus drew gently to the No.5 stop outside the entrance to departures, he alighted, waiting for the other five or so passengers to go before him and there, by the stop sign, was a bin with a gaping hole in the side for recyclables.

Wrapping his handkerchief around its handle, he removed the pistol, wiping it clean as best and as unobtrusively as he could, and dropped it into the bin. He was pretty confident no-one had taken any notice of what he was doing.

His flight left in just over an hour.

CHAPTER 49

Everything unfolded in slowtime. One minute they were laughing at Robin's victory in their silly game, the next she was there, face down, in the water, being buffeted by the waves but apparently unmoving.

He didn't think. He dropped his glass. Instinct drove him as he dived into the murky water towards her. Although a strong swimmer, he struggled against the two-foot waves, caused by the wake of the cruise liner, hitting the quayside, lapping over the edges. Eventually, he reached her, still face down. He wrenched her over. Her face was grey. He manoeuvred behind her, and wrapping an arm about her chest, keeping her head above water, he paddled, as best he could, towards the quay.

There, Raffaello and his fellow-waiter Max, who'd both been serving the quayside tables when it happened, were on their knees by the docking post, arms outstretched, willing William to hand her to them.

As William neared the quay, Raff was able to grab hold of her dress at her shoulder and Max somehow secured her arm. Between them, they managed to drag her, face down, up onto the quay.

It was then, while still in the water, that William saw the red stain on the back of her dress.

And although it occurred only in the recesses of his brain, he registered, somewhere in the crowd behind Robin, back to him, moving away, a familiar shape.

Ricardo, *Chez Nico's* owner, had called both the police and the 112 ambulance service when he'd seen what had happened.

Max and Raff managed to drag William from the water and there he lay, propped on an elbow beside Robin, summoning the strength and the air to get to his knees and there to administer CPR.

Robin lay unmoving beside him. Still a ghostly grey, she appeared not to be breathing. He struggled to his knees and started the procedure: thirty compressions, two rescue breaths, thirty compressions, two rescue breaths – no response – thirty compressions, two rescue breaths.

It seemed he had only just started when a firm hand on his shoulder gently pulled him away from Robin. He was about to panic when he saw the uniform of the paramedic.

He had not heard the siren of the *ambulanza*, had not noticed the two medics carrying the stretcher up onto the dock. But now he saw a *polizia* launch arriving, its blue lights flashing.

An oxygen mask had been placed over Robin's face and the chest compressions the paramedic had continued to administer seemed to be working. Robin had spluttered into the mask, which was quickly removed, and she appeared now to be breathing unaided.

She was gently lifted and strapped onto the stretcher and passed expertly over the quayside edge down into the *ambulanza* where she was received by the driver, assisted by the second paramedic who had jumped nimbly into the boat to help. They had clearly done something like this many times before.

Before he had to ask, William too was helped into the boat which took off at speed in the direction of the Ospedale SS. Giovanni e Paolo. In Veneziano: *Zani Polo*, Venice's Ospedale Civile, to the *pronto soccorso*, the emergency entrance, on the Fondamenta

Nuove on the north of the island.

By now, as the boat sped along, Robin had regained some of her colour and her breathing appeared to be steady. William sat by her side, distraught to see her in such a state.

She opened her eyes and, with obvious effort, reached for his hand.

'Forgive me, my love,' she said, before her hand dropped away and her eyes closed again.

The medic moved William to the stern of the boat and, occupying his seat, placed the oxygen mask back over Robin's face while he monitored her pulse.

'We'll be there in two or three minutes,' said the other paramedic in perfectly accented English. William nodded.

◆ ◆ ◆

They'd removed William's wet clothes, put him in a room to dry off, given him hospital pyjamas and a rough dressing gown to wear and hotel slippers and then insisted he take the antibiotics. He protested. There was nothing wrong with him, he told them in his fluent Veneziano. They were surprised but happy to carry the conversation on in the local dialect.

'There will be if you don't take these,' said the nurse, smiling, holding two bright red pills in her hand. 'It's E-coli soup out there in the canal.'

William took the pills without further ado.

He sat miserably in a corridor for four hours, waiting for news of Robin, all manner of dread imaginings going through his brain. What nagged him most was her plea, in the *ambulanza*, for forgiveness. What on earth could that mean?

During that time he had been interviewed by the police.

He was surprised that they knew who he was – he'd never

adjusted to, indeed, he had actively resisted, his unwelcome fame – but was gratified that they knew nothing of Robin. Although utterly miserable, he rehearsed the story of the death threats, the accidental death of the kitchen staff, and their escape, for the second time, to his apartment in Venice.

He was confident, he told them, that it was impossible that the killer could know they were here. And to their quizzically-raised eyebrows, he had no answer. Indeed, a dawning realization swept over him that he and Robin may have been rash in their imagined security in Venice.

He gave them DI Barcley's name and suggested that they might like to call him for confirmation; although he doubted that Barcley would be able to afford them any particular insights into what had happened.

The policemen were thoughtful, gentle and possessed an acuity that William had not seen in anyone from Thames Valley Police. They left him with their hopes for Robin's full recovery, to sit alone in the astringent corridor, smelling unpleasantly of solvents he could not recognize, in despair.

◆ ◆ ◆

He was exhausted, nodding off to sleep, his chin near his chest, when a middle-aged man in green scrubs and with a kindly smile gently nudged him awake.

'*Signore Adams*?'

'*Si.*'

They continued the conversation in Italian, William lapsing into Veneziano when he realized that the doctor was Venetian.

'She's been shot in the back,' said Dottore Fanucci, '*ma niente di preoccupante*, there's nothing to worry about, she'll be fine.'

William was not reassured; he'd heard that kind of thing before.

'Tell me exactly what you've done and what the prognosis is.' He was now vitally alert.

'A bullet ... no, that's not quite right, a pellet: it was a curious thing. I've never seen anything like it before. A strange material and unusual shape. The police are examining it now. It entered through the back, between the sixth and seventh rib, missing both of them, thank goodness, and pierced her lung, where it lodged. It's what we call traumatic intercostal pneumothorax.

'We did a thoracoscopy: put a tube in her upper chest to release the trapped air escaping from the collapsed lung ... she'd been in the water a long time. The escaped air was pushing her heart and other lung against her chest wall. Had we not got to her in time, the air pressure would have forced both organs to collapse.

'The tube we inserted is attached to a pump to remove the excess air and relieve the pressure on her collapsed lung. It allows for safe decompression.

'I made a cut into her back, from the site of the entry of the pellet, and, having removed it, then closed the wound. She was lucky it had not gone out the other side. I suppose it had to do with the odd nature of the pellet ... not being able to penetrate, I mean.

'Anyway, we closed up her lung. I did a little local pleurodesis – stuck that part of her lung to her chest wall so that it could not collapse again – and cleaned up the wound.

'Unfortunately, she'd ingested quite a lot of canal water, and doubtless some had got into her lung through the wound. Not a good set of bugs to introduce to a healthy environment through a wound. But we're feeding her industrial strength antibiotics to combat the bacteria through her saline drip and she's on full maintenance monitoring.

'*Deo volente*, she'll be fine in a day or two and back to normal in a couple of weeks.'

'May I see her?'

'She's just had major surgery. She's heavily sedated. There is no way she will be awake before the morning. I suggest you go home and come back here at nine,' and then, looking at the hospital kit William was wearing, 'I'll have them get your clothes.'

William was mightily relieved, having been given his now-dry clothes back, to discover his wallet, keys and mobile phone neatly placed on top of his dry, folded clothes, presented to him by the same nurse who had fed him the antibiotics. Clearly they had survived his immersion in the Guidecca Canal in the tight back and front pockets of his trousers. Although he doubted that his phone would work again.

The walk home was only fifteen minutes and he was relieved, on arrival, to find that Nonna Claudia was there to greet him. Someone from the Ospedale must have contacted her to tell her what had happened. He was reminded that, when the tourists were discounted, Venice was a small town.

Nonna fed him, plied him with generous amounts of health-giving cabernet franc, one of his favourite grapes, and ushered him into bed as if he were, in fact, her grandchild. He was ever so grateful.

He fell into a deep, troubled, sleep in which images of Robin coursed painfully through his mind, each ending with her anguished plea: *forgive me.*

CHAPTER 50

His return to England was uneventful. But his deep-seated unhappiness grew in inverse proportion to the mundanity of all about him. He could think of little but his monumental failures: killing three innocent men and now killing the wrong person from a mere twelve feet or so. And on top of that, he'd lost his rucksack with his book that may, or may not, have had his name in it. He might as well have left a calling card.

And then there was the gun in the bin. He'd disposed of it so quickly and in such fear of discovery that now he began to feel certain that he'd left prints on it, somewhere. Maybe when he was loading it … He'd hardly had the chance to wipe it thoroughly.

He decided that he had left a trail so clear that even a child could expose him.

As a child, he'd worshipped his mother. She had given him to believe that she, too, adored him. He admired the bitterness she carried about: its focus, the way it empowered her, the manner in which it informed her being. She seemed to him to be relentless in the way she manipulated the world about her to achieve her goals. He had decided, at an early age, that he would emulate her as best he could; he would wield what influence he could to bend the world in his service; he would use his God-given gifts as acutely as he might to achieve fame and fortune.

He had decided on his goal at quite a young age and had pursued it relentlessly, making enormous intellectual strides and establishing a name for himself, until, that is, Adams had brought his edifice of painstakingly developed achievement crumbling down around him.

Of course, his only option was to kill the man who had brought him low and debased his life's work. It was only too appropriate that he should poison Adams, as his mother had poisoned her abusive husband before him.

But that, through no fault of his own, had come to grief. And now he had failed in the simple matter of shooting the shit at close range. What's more, he had left a trail as wide as a highway to his own front door.

He sat in his study, in despair, drinking himself into stupefaction.

CHAPTER 51

Sam Wilson paid £400 for a picture taken on a smartphone of Robin Atwell lying, arms splayed, face down in the Guidecca Canal, her body rising on the crest of a small wave caused by a cruise liner, clearly visible in the background of the shot. He would have paid twice that much. The picture was perfect.

The photograph headed his *Oxford Intrigues* column, which had been flagging of late since the stars of the column had vanished, again, into thin air.

But now he knew. They were hiding out in Venice. He had flown there the day he had received the picture from a regular reader of his column who was holidaying in Venice and happened to be on the scene. She was happy to be interviewed, giving a blow-by-blow description of what she'd witnessed.

The Venetian police, once he'd managed to track down the appropriate authorities from amongst the *Polizia Nazionale,* the *Carabinieri,* the *Polizia Municipale,* the *Polizia Provinciale,* the *Polizia di Stato,* the *Guardia di Finanza,* the *Vigili Urbani,* and the *Polizia Locale,* which turned out to be the ones he wanted.

And while getting an appointment with Commissario Saltuario in the *stazione* in Castello was straightforward enough, he soon discovered that the Commissario did not speak English or, more likely as he suspected, pretended not to speak English. Their meeting was short, fruitless and a complete waste of his time.

Not so futile was his interview with Raff, Max and Ricardo of *Chez Nico*. All were happy to talk to him in the hope that the publicity might bring an attempted murderer to justice, at least that's the way he sold it to them. Ricardo, as owner of the bar, was not uninterested in the publicity it might bring to the bar as well.

They described the whole episode in detail, their own part in it, together with what they knew of the English *signore* and *signorina* with whom they had become friends.

Wilson used this familial angle in his new column piece to tug at his readers' heartstrings: friendly English couple, trying to escape an unhinged killer after their blood, rescued by charming Italian waiters who risked their own lives (a twist Wilson added to spice up the story) to drag them both out of the water to safety.

It was precisely this article that DI Barcley now read at his desk in the Oxford station of Thames Valley Police. He had just got off the phone from Venice, having spoken with his opposite number there, Commissario Saltuario, who spoke remarkably good English, and who had told him of all that had transpired. The *Polizia Locale* had no clues, no suspects, no witnesses who'd seen Dr Atwell shot. But the waiters at the bar, *Chez Nico*, did say they'd served a man who left his bag on a chair, to go to the toilet they assumed, and after the kerfuffle was all over saw that he'd not touched his drink, which was unusual, and that his bag and he were gone by the time they got back to work, having helped Robin and William out of the water. But no, neither could remember anything about him. In fact, it was probably not relevant.

Saltuario was apologetic that he could not be of more help and, of course, if anything came to light he would let Barcley know. In the meantime, his officers would look in on the couple occasionally when doing their rounds, once she had been released from hospital. At present, there was an officer stationed by her room in the hospital, as was standard procedure after an attempted murder.

CHAPTER 52

It was good at first to talk with Claire; he felt isolated, lacking confidence, insecure. He was happy to hear her voice and was reassured until, through his worry, he eventually caught the tentative timbre of her intonation, her concern at the other end of the line.

'What's wrong, Claire?' he asked, warily, detecting her hesitation.

Her news that Larry was dead shook him to the core.

While initially she had kept Larry's death from him, the time had come when she could no longer forebear. Given all the news generated about everything surrounding the lives of William and Robin, it was only too possible that he might hear from some other source. She was determined that if he was going to learn of recent events, it should be from her, although the prospect of informing him, and causing him pain, distressed her.

She rehearsed all the details as she'd been given them by Barcley: not long after his return from Paris, Larry had hanged himself (she didn't go into detail about the manner of his hanging: that, had he stood on his tiptoes, he could have stopped the slow strangulation, such was his apparent desperation to die); the coroner had said that analysis of his stomach contents confirmed that he had not, in the week prior to his death at least, taken his medication and this, the forensic pathologist had confirmed, was enough to push him to suicide; that his parents had, once the body was released, returned to the States, there to bury him; that they blamed William for his death. Claire felt she could not hide this gruesome detail from William in that, on her desk, she had a letter, clearly from the Veritys, which she knew in her bones would be dripping with the venom they had poured on William at the inquest. She had not yet decided, as she would do later, to dispose of the missive.

Again, he felt the black hand of despair dragging him down into the depths of his soul, to a place where no hope shone in his darkness. A place he'd known only too well with Gill and Jeny's deaths.

And although it did not ameliorate his hopelessness, Claire's call to William was, in part at least, not all bad: he desperately needed some good news.

After the tragedy of Larry Verity's death, the SENDIST tribunal had decided, following extensive representations from the Provost of Oriel College Oxford, that there was no case to answer. Indeed, Prof William Adams had shown great forbearance under the circumstances and had, at all times, acted not just professionally, but caringly. This was confirmed by Father Penrose, Oriel's Chaplain, who had seen Larry several times a week, at Larry's request, until his departure for Paris, and who felt, now that Larry was dead, unconstrained by the bonds of confidentiality: Larry had been clear that the Prof, as he called William, had been patient with him, had put up with his odd behaviour, and had given him a lot of leeway.

Doubtless sensitive to Larry's mourning parents, the presiding judge did not say outright that the petition was vexatious but, with due diligence, sensitivity, and appropriate equivocation, she said something similar.

It was only after Claire had read the full judgement to William over the phone, that he realised how much the strain of this, together with Robin's attempted murder, was bearing upon him.

He was not sure that he could take any more. It was only the prospect of Robin's recovery and the joy of their relationship, unimpeded by murderers or madmen, that kept him going.

William spent as much time in the hospital as they would allow him. But he used his time at the apartment to take stock. He could not bear the thought of sketching; he resisted Nonna's attempts to coddle him; he had no desire to walk the calli of Venice alone; he ate little and at nearby bars, such was his concern for Robin's recovery but also the jeopardy in which he'd put her.

Robin's hospital stay reminded him of Gill's last days and compounded his upset for her recovery.

What on earth was he to do?

He felt that he could make no plans until this threat, hanging over their heads, was lifted. Was the murderer still in Venice? Should they return to England? Where could they be safe? He could not bear the thought of putting Robin in danger again but was bereft of any clear plan of how he might shield her from harm.

All he knew was that he loved her desperately and wanted to be with her, safe, protected and happy.

CHAPTER 53

Dottore Fannuci was proved right: Robin's recovery was fast. Whatever drugs it was they administered had returned her to a smiling equanimity with a celerity that William could not have dreamed possible. Her colour had returned, her outlook was sunny, in spite of what she had been through. And although she complained of how demanding they were, the physios had her up and about, almost walking normally, by day two. William could not have been happier with her progress.

On the condition that she returned to the Ospedale daily, for one week, for physiotherapy, Robin was released on day four.

As they returned to the apartment, hospital bag in hand, Nonna lurched, about to embrace her in the usual bear hug, when William intervened to remind her that Robin's back remained tender and would be for some weeks to come. Instead, Nonna kissed her firmly on the lips, hands on both cheeks, with tears in her eyes.

It was lunchtime and she had prepared typical Venetian dishes to celebrate Robin's homecoming: *Tagliolini Neri alle Mazzancolle*, black tagliolini with prawns, asparagus and peas, followed by *Baccalà alla Vicentina*, dried cod in a Vicenza style sauce. William had splashed out on a Ronco del Gnemiz, 2011, to celebrate her return.

Nonna was unusually circumspect in departing soon after their arrival, leaving them alone to enjoy the privacy of what she knew was an important moment in their lives. Secretly, she had been hoping that William would use the opportunity to propose. Nonna was of the age of women who could not understand that any woman could be complete, or happy, unless she was married. And in spite of seeing many marriages break down, some of her friends and contemporaries included, she held firmly to her belief in the centrality of marriage, and of course children, the more, the better, in a woman's life.

'I can't begin to tell you how happy I am to have you back, safe and sound,' he said as they clinked glasses in a silent toast.

'As am I,' she said, but with a note of caution in her tone. 'But … well … I didn't have anything much to do in hospital but think. And I've been thinking …'

William was beginning to worry. 'Yes?'

'Well … whoever tried to kill me was … I don't really know how to put this. I think it was not me they were after. I think they were trying to kill you and I just, sort of, got in the way.'

William was becoming distraught at what might follow, at the implications of what she was saying.

'I agree,' he said in deep sadness.

'Let me just say my piece,' she was a little too curt. William worried even more at what was coming. 'I don't know what the answer is but I know that we're both still in danger. For all we know, he could be still here. He might even be watching us now. We are not going to be safe until he is caught.

'Do you remember that, when you got the last note, the one about Thermopylae, that you suggested that I would be better off if I wasn't around you?'

'Yes,' he said, dejection setting in. He could see where this was going.

'Well, I've come to the conclusion that you were right.'

'Oh …' He knew she was right, but the pain that the recognition brought him was unbearable. He knew he was just too toxic to be around. He prepared himself for the inevitable.

'But I've decided, equally, that I can't live without you. I don't *want* to live without you.'

William was flummoxed. Where was she leading?

'So … William Adams. Will you marry me?'

Tears flowed freely down his face as he enveloped her in his arms as firmly as her wound would allow. He was irrepressibly happy but his brain roiled with the implications of what she had said.

'But what are we going to do with this threat hanging over our heads? How can we guarantee our security? Should we even be staying here?' he asked.

'I'll take that as a "no" then, shall I?'

Then he realized. He'd been so overwhelmed by her proposal. So confused by where she might be leading. Still so concerned for her well-being, that he'd not answered her question.

'I love you, Robin. Of course I'll marry you. I thought you'd never ask,' he joked, as much to relieve his own pent up emotion as anything else.

Again they embraced. This kiss, he knew, he would remember for ever.

Over Nonna's scrummy meal, they made plans, squirreling out the implications of their complex and burdensome circumstances.

'I've been thinking, too,' he said. 'I've spoken with the police while you've been convalescing and they have no further clues about the killer. They've contacted Barcley, who's been useless, as you would expect, but at least he's filled them in on what's happened at home.

'I think we have no choice but to go home …'

'I've started to think of *this* as home,' she said, taking in the sweep of Venice in her arms.

'I know. And maybe it can be in the future. But until this horror is sorted, we need, I think, to go back.' He avoided using the word 'home'.

'The Venetian police will not provide security …'

'But nor will Thames Valley Police,' she interrupted.

'I know … I know. But they don't have to. As I said, I've been thinking about this. And frankly, I don't know why it hasn't occurred before. I suppose I've just got used to our life, cocooned in College, away from the cares of the world …'

'You're rambling, my love.'

'Sorry … yes. Although Thames Valley Police won't provide protection, there's no earthly reason why we can't provide it ourselves. I can pay for us to be shielded against all odds. I don't know why I didn't think of it earlier.

'Claire has bought the house in Summertown. We could move there. It's possible it would take the killer sometime to find us. But we could settle in there with the highest levels of security possible and endure it until this bastard is caught. I have to believe that it wouldn't take too long.'

Over Nonna's mouthwatering meal, they discussed at length the implications of William employing a security firm to guard them, such was their concern for their future. No doubt, such a firm could also establish a parallel investigation and try to catch the killer.

At last, William realized that they had just been engaged and they had said nothing of the wedding: when, where, how …

They talked well into the afternoon, At one point, because it had been niggling at him so, he asked Robin: 'Do you remember the *ambulanza* ride to the hospital?'

'Not really. I was pretty out of it.'

'On the way, you took hold of my hand …'

'Yes. I vaguely remember …'

'And you said: "Forgive me, my love". Do you remember?'

'Honestly … no. I was hardly *compos mentis*.'

'It's plagued me ever since. What on earth could there be that I need to forgive you for?' He was clearly anguished.

'Nothing, darling. It was no doubt the delirium speaking.'

And with that, she took his hand and led him to the bedroom.

'What on earth are you doing?' he asked, incredulously.

'Isn't it obvious?'

'Yes. But …'

'But what? We've just got engaged. Don't you think we should celebrate?'

'Yes. But … your back.'

'I don't have to lie on my back for us to "celebrate",' she said as they stood by the bed. Never had she looked so sexy.

And with that she instructed him, in minute detail, how best to remove her clothes so as to avoid causing any discomfort. He did exactly as he was told.

She then removed his clothes, slowly, gingerly, restricting her movements so as not to cause, as she called it, a twitch.

'I see that not all of you objects to my plans at seduction,' she said, reaching down to hold his erection.

And still holding it, she guided him onto the bed, gently climbing over his supine body, manoeuvring him into her and nuzzling her groin into his. She sat there, glorious in her exquisite nudity, looking down at him with a love he found breathtaking.

She moved, a gentle rolling, to and fro, across his loins.

For a brief moment, all thoughts of death, drowning and despair were replaced by desire and hope, bringing their love to fruition.

◆ ◆ ◆

They agreed, that once she was fit for travel, they would return to the UK. Claire had already been asked to arrange round-the-clock security cover for them.

CHAPTER 54

Sunday, 30th June

First Sunday since 'escape' from Ospedale.

Walked to Frari via breakfast at Impronta. Luciana and Julia most solicitous; they'd seen it all on the news. Apparently, I'm quite a celebrity in Il Gazzettino, or at least I was for 15 mins.

Long service, with children taking their first communion. Very moving.

Home for lunch. W. doing all the cooking now that I'm an invalid.

Felt quite tired after our excursion so rested in the afternoon.

Went to S. Trovaso for an evening concert. French choir singing Mozart's Requiem. Not quite Oxford standard.

Light dinner.

Monday, 1st July

Feeling <u>so</u> much better today!

From Impronta breakfast to Goldini's house on the way to Rialto. W. won't let me shop. I'm being spoiled rotten. Loving it!

Goldini disappointing: limited/poor display. He's certainly not the Venetian Shakespeare as billed!

On to S. Polo Apostoli. Glorious Tintoretto Ultima Cena + Tiepolo (the younger) stations of the cross in the Oratory.

On to Giacomo dell'Olio with its curious offering: Lotto altarpiece (Madonna il trono) too far away to see properly. 4th C Byzantine column, 'new' chapel with Veronese ceiling and Bassanos and Tintorettos with Palmas (we've decided Palma is a bit like chips – he goes with everything).

Salad lunch at home.

Bitta for dinner. Super meal. I had three courses!

Tuesday, 2nd July

Think I might have overdone things a bit yesterday.

Went to hospital first thing to have my dressing changed. So pleased, they removed the stitches (12). W. tells me that, like me, my scar is lovely!

Caught the vap. to Ferrovia & bought tickets for Vicenza tomorrow. Thence to Cannaregio to S. Giobbe (I didn't know Job was a saint. Maybe it's an Italian thing).

Church plain single nave – chancel swathed in plastic. Lombardo altarpiece and Robbia majolica (4 evangelists + God) – most unusual.

Then to S. Alvise (high altar also in plastic therefore missing Tiepolo Deposition). Strange painted trompe l'oeil on flat roof in very unGothic style. (W. intrigued).

Scary screens to imprison nuns of the adjoining convent.

Stilted but colourful Bastianis and 2 Tiepolos: Flagellation & Crowning with Thorns. Not my kind of religion.

In the light of tomorrow, home early. W. is cooking Pollo alla Buranea. Smells heavenly.

Wednesday, 3rd July

Rise at 6.15 to catch the 7.34 to Vicenza. Swift walk to the station, Impronta for coffee on the way.

Arrive at Vicenza at 9.00 and walk to the centre. Visit Raffaello versus Picasso (!) exhibition at Basilica Palladiana. It was a wonder: paintings included Bellini, Giorgione (W. thinks not his), Titian,

Bacon, Renoir & Freud ...

We were both amazed and thrilled to see so many favourites and pictures we had not seen before. Not sure why Raffaello mentioned in the title as no paintings by him ...

My best: a Guercino Madonna con Bambino. I have never seen such a beautiful child, nor such a tender rendition of motherhood. This, of all the paintings I have ever seen, moved me to tears. Came over all maternal; best not to tell W.

Then walked to Teatro Olimipico then Palazzo Chiemicati.

Lunch at an excellent Osteria then to the Palladio Museum and walk around the streets to see some of his houses. Then to Duomo and Museo Diocesaro.

Home to noisy Venice on 16.34. Pizza for dinner. W. got v. wet getting it!

A perfect day.

Thursday, 4th July

Decided yesterday, on the train back home, to return to Blighty today. Claire ordered the jet so we left Venice at 15.50. Home by 19.00.

In the light of present circumstances, Claire has booked us into the Randolph. Barcley was waiting on the steps when we arrived! Hearts sank.

Claire has booked an entire floor for us! Security guards everywhere: one on steps at arrival, one behind front reception, one accompanying us in lift – apparently our personal minder – one each at stairs between floors and two outside the door to our suite. Our minder planned on settling into the lounge of our suite but W. gave him short shrift.

I couldn't bear this for long, but have not complained. W. has got enough on his mind. At least we feel safe!

Dinner served in room. Nothing like the quality of food W. has been *cooking me! And will have early night.*

After yesterday's excursion to Vicenza am buggered. Hope for a quiet day tomorrow.

◆ ◆ ◆

It was two days later that their lives took a sudden turn.

CHAPTER 55

As an employee, Jack Sutherland had been fastidious: he'd always sought permission for absences; always advised the office when he was out on business, official or otherwise; always proved punctual in keeping office hours, often working far longer than might reasonably be expected of him.

So it was his absence of four days that had led to James Southwell's concerned calls to his home number – all unanswered – and, eventually to the police.

It was this call, coupled with that of a neighbour in his block of flats five days later about an unpleasant smell in the corridor outside his apartment, together with the fact that he was a colleague of William Adams, that led the police, under the direction of DI Barcley, to force entry to his Woodstock Road address on the Thursday morning of the neighbour's call.

It was later estimated by the pathologist that death had occurred the previous Friday evening. It was only after the body had been removed to the morgue, on the day after they'd gained entry, that William Adams accompanied DI Barcley and his sergeant to the flat where they asked him to help them make sense of what they'd discovered.

As they entered the apartment, William detected the unpleasant odour, in spite of the fact that all the windows and doors to the property were wide open. He nodded to the officer on duty at the front door as they entered.

On the book-lined wall, to the left of the desk with its huge computer, were two whole shelves of A4 box files, each marked with Roman numerals, after the single word: *Meroitic*. Fifty three files in all: I – LIII.

William was astonished. He opened the file marked *Meroitic* I and found the first entry, dated July, 2003. By his rough calculation, Sutherland would have been about 19 years-old at the time.

It did not take him long, dipping in and out of other files, all meticulously dated, annotated and cross-referenced, to establish that the files ran in chronological order. The last entry in the final file, *Meroitic* LIII, was dated roughly three years ago. Almost to the day *The Times* had made public the announcement that William Adams had cracked the Nubian language of Meroitic. A clipping of that very notice was attached to the second-to-last page in the file; it had been scored in red biro in curious slashes and exclamations. The page following it was incoherent gobbledegook.

A closer examination of earlier files revealed a prolonged and systematic attempt on Sutherland's part to crack the language.

Indeed, over the days that followed, William was able to establish Jack's *modus operandi*: ancient Semitic languages are all written with consonants only, the spoken vowels consistently ignored and omitted, as in, for example, modern Hebrew. The definite and indefinite articles were also left out. The key to cracking or translating Semitic languages depended on the form or tense of the verb, in which the subject, sometimes a noun, sometimes a suffix, was added to the signs expressing the verbal notion. In Classical Egyptian, this was known as the *sdm.f* form. Because this form excluded almost any English tense or mood, even the simplest translation required a new mind-set which most found difficult.

Jack's investigations were predicated on the three-consonant verb-form base but one which rang different changes through declension and tense. A completely wrong-headed idea. But one which, until William's discovery, was not without merit.

Since Jack was nineteen, presumably his second year of reading Egyptology at the University of Liverpool, he had rigorously and meticulously beavered away at this singular attempt at decipherment of this ancient language.

It was a work of extraordinary and outstanding scholarship.

And it was a monumental failure.

William's own work established that Meroitic sat on the fault line between the northern plate of Semitic Egyptian and the southern plate of Hamitic African.

Jack had tried, for twenty years, to establish that Meroitic was a language falling purely within the northern, Semitic plate. And he had failed.

Although his life's work doubtless offered insights into the functioning and development of Semitic tongues, itself worthy of publication in books and articles in learned journals, William's own discovery had thwarted his endeavours, robbing him of the fame that was heaped in abundance on Prof William Adams.

Here was reason enough to determine that Jack Sutherland was the attempted murderer of William Adams but also the unwitting killer of three, innocent kitchen staff at Oriel College, and also the man who had shot Robin in Venice.

'Oh,' said Barcley, 'and we found this.' He handed William a pro forma application for membership of the Taylorian Library, sent from Princeton and dated before Larry had arrived in Oxford. Next to 'NAME:' was typed 'CLARENCE EVAN VERITY'.

'One of Sutherland's jobs at the Institute was to confirm applications for the use of the library. This explains where he got the idea for the first death note you received,' said Barcley. 'It would appear that its arrival, nominating you as his supervisor, gave Sutherland the idea to use it in the note. He wanted to demean your achievement by calling it 'clever', but thought a clever way to do this would be to disguise it by condensing Larry's name. It was, after all, a tragic coincidence.'

It was the first time in the entire investigation, thought William, that Barcley had discovered anything of consequence and drawn a reasonable conclusion from it.

William said nothing.

◆ ◆ ◆

Analysis of Jack's computer's hard drive revealed that he had hacked into William's correspondence with Claire; that he was indeed the author of the three anonymous notes – death threats – to William Adams; that he had accessed the dark web via TOR to purchase a 3D processed composite gun and bullets, together with two shipments of aconite; that he had purchased a passport and three easyJet return tickets to Venice where he had stayed, on each occasion, at the same Air B&B.

One of the most recent entries on the hard drive was one such poison purchase. It was not stretching deduction too far to conclude – as was now confirmed by the coroner – that it was his ingestion of the second shipment of aconite that led to Jack's death.

Slowly, they pieced together the events leading to Jack's demise: not long after Robin had been shot (now understood clearly to be a bungled attempt on William's life), he had purchased a second dose of poison over the dark web.

Having finished work at 5.00pm on the Friday, he had gone home where he had eaten an Indian takeaway meal from a restaurant a few doors down from his flat. He had then consumed well over half a bottle of very expensive Japanese whisky and had then taken the aconite.

Death was virtually instantaneous.

He left no suicide note; offered no apology or contrition for his abominable actions.

It had been William's unpleasant duty to scour through Jack's *Meroitic* files. On the basis of his discoveries there, together with other comments from the hard drive of oblique references here, snippets of clues there, William's researches led to a case file being opened for a murder investigation into the death of Samuel Sutherland, Jack's father. The body was to be exhumed with a view to determine whether the cause of death was, in fact, poisoning and not the heart attack recorded on the death certificate. Jack's 89 year-old mother was the only suspect.

Jack's *Meroitic* files, once they no longer served as evidence, had been transported to the Taylor Institute where they were temporarily stored, due to a shortage of space, ironically, in Jack's old office. It was agreed that they were of considerable value in furthering the study of the history of Meroë and Napatan but also more generally in the field of Egyptology.

William declined James' offer to sift through them with a view to publishing the academic insights they contained.

CHAPTER 56

They had decided, having fallen in love with the place, that they would formally seal their engagement on Torcello.

From Oxford, they'd made a brief excursion to London to buy a ring and it was on this small, unruly island where the city of Venice began its life that they would formalize their commitment.

Established in the fifth and sixth centuries, Torcello, a sprawling, marshy island was originally a city of palaces and churches and a population of 20,000. Roman citizens of the mainland town of Altina, escaping the barbarian raids by Attila and his Huns, had escaped here. Now, the number living on the island was below 60, silted canals and malaria having taken their toll. Even the Bishop of Torcello chose to live on nearby Murano. The greatest vestige of the once bustling Torcello is the magnificent Byzantine cathedral and its nearby church of Santa Fosca, reminding William of Istanbul's Santa Sophia.

The walk from the vaporetto stop to the basilica is almost half a mile, over the Devil's bridge with the campanile of the cathedral of Santa Maria Assunta dominating the skyline. The sun had yet to burn the morning dew off the untamed plant life by the path and there was still a morning crispness in the air. There were few people about at this hour. They took their time, not wishing to defer the engagement but to savour every moment of this beautiful day.

Having spent half an hour in the Museo over mosaics, icons, seals and *bocche di leone*, open lions' mouths for posting letters of denunciation of one's fellow citizens – a legalized form of grudge-taking – *contra la sanita per il città de Torcello*, they moved across the open square, past the fifth century throne of Attila, and into the cathedral.

The oldest building in the Laguna, dating from 638, Santa Maria is imposing. But the main reason they had come was the west end mosaic in the form of a Last Judgement. The picture covered the entire West wall, about three storeys high and thirty feet across. The shimmering scene, overwhelmingly in gold tesserae, commanded their attention as it did all who came here. Although the scene was designed to strike fear into the hearts of all who saw it, William found it strangely comforting.

'It's about eleventh century. Some have drawn comparisons with Dante's *Divine Comedy*, which he was writing about the same time,' he said, 'although it's quite overpowering, I find it reassuring: it reminds me of my mortality, my weakness. The wages of my sins, if you like.'

'There's nothing remotely sinful about you,' Robin protested.

'You'd be surprized.'

'Yes. I would. But do you believe in all this life after death business?'

'I'd like to. I mean, I'm drawn to it. But my problem is that I just can't make *sense* of it: the idea of a disembodied post-mortem survival logically depends on the view that having a body is not essential for identifying a person. But that, I'm afraid, just can't be true.

'So, no: my head tells me there is no life after death, but my heart wants me to hope for it.'

'You're such a romantic,' she said, always amazed at what a complex character he was.

'Speaking of which,' he said, going down on one knee and

producing the ring – a single large sapphire surrounded by diamonds - he had bought. 'Robin Jane Atwell, will you marry me?' he asked, as thousands of saints and sinners looked down on them both from the glimmering mosaic behind them. 'I can promise to love and adore you as long as I breathe, if you'll let me.'

'I will,' she said, lifting him into her arms and, in front of God and his holy angels, she planted a generous kiss on his willing lips, much to the consternation of other couples now slowly filling the golden nave.

Robin could not help herself. As they strolled to the Locanda Cipriani for a celebratory lunch, she kept glancing at the ring, feeling the delicious unreality of her new status as an officially engaged woman.

She could not have imagined, all that time ago, that the man she had stormed out on in The Bear and Ragged Staff would end up being her husband. They'd set a date for February, six months should be enough time to prepare for the wedding.

CHAPTER 57

'I'll have a dry Manhattan, with bourbon, shaken, no twist and two maraschino cherries, please,' said William.

'I'll have a Bellini.'

'Of course, Madam.'

'I'll have a gin and tonic, Bombay Sapphire, make it a double, if you would.'

'I'll just have a sip of his,' said Anne.

The restaurant, one of Venice's finest, is on the top floor of the Danieli, overlooking the Palladian island church of San Giorgio Maggiore. The quiet waters of the Giudecca Canal sparkled the reflections of Schiavonni's lights and the channel lamps of the Laguna.

Ross and Anne Farnsom had joined William and Robin for a two week stay in the city and the Veneto; they planned day trips to Padua, Verona, Vicenza and maybe even further afield.

The Elkins were unable to join them: Anthony's blood pressure remained worryingly high, his dietary indolence even higher, and Ross had advised him not to travel.

Robin had fallen in love with the Farnsoms instantly. William had already told her so much about his best man and his wife, and Anne and Robin had started up an immediate friendship. Robin felt as if she'd known them both for years.

'Tomorrow,' said William, 'we'll catch a vaporetto to Torcello and we'll lunch outdoors at Locanda Cipriani. You'll both love it.'

The Farnsoms had arrived from Australia two days before and William was anxious to share his favourite places with them.

Ross had had to expand his practice, taking on new cardiologists to keep up with the demand after the additional fame into which he'd been thrust following his involvement in William's Australian adventures and the subsequent tragedy of Gill's death. He was only now winding down following the flight from Sydney and the frenetic demands of 'healing the damn sick' as he was wont, affectionately, to say.

His friendship with William he resumed with ease, as if they'd not been separated all those months of turmoil for both men.

The next day they would return to Torcello, the place where, the week before, William had formally proposed to Robin.

◆ ◆ ◆

They sat in the shade in a rough grass area outside the restaurant proper. While less polished and less expensive than its Guidecca name-sake, the Locanda Cipriani's food and wine list was every bit as good.

'Same play, different actors,' said Ross. He was referring to the fact that both men had been chided by their respective partners for already being too well-lubricated to have ordered yet another bottle of the Grange Bin 95, the only Australian wine on the list and one Ross had insisted they order. 1998 was a great year, he assured them.

'My father used to say it to explain the fact that we all face the same, or similar, existential conditions. Whether in respect of our own aspirations or failures, or in respect of the way we deal with them: same play, different actors,' said Ross.

'Although, to be honest, he always meant it as a joke: he would use it gently to chide my mother when she rather predictably got at him for one of his failings or other. His best mate's wife, Molly, was prone to the same sort of nagging of her husband George, and it amused him.'

'I would like to think,' said William, surprised at Ross' unusual flight of philosophical fancy, 'that the play is different for us all and that it's our reaction to what life dishes up to us that shows there's a certain sameness in our nature.

'I think its that level of empathy that binds us together, makes us one.

'So maybe it's also: different play, same actors?'

By now, both women were rolling their eyes.

AFTERWORD

Discerning readers will be aware that I have jerrymandered history to suit my purposes and for that I apologize. The Taylor Institute is, indeed, dedicated to the languages of Europe and not to those of Egypt and the Ancient Near East. Sir Flinders Petrie did all I credited him with but it was, in fact, at the University of London that he occupied the first Chair of Egyptology in the UK.

Likewise, Sir Alan Gardiner's achievements are accurately described but he, too, was not based at the Taylorian. Nor was the Egypt Exploaration Society located there. It is simply too good a location, opposite The Randolph, not far from Oriel College and near William's favourite restaurants, for me to resist the temptation to place him there.

I have portrayed Venice as accurately as I can remember from the time that we lived there, twelve years ago. *Chez Nico* serves a fabulous Campari spritz.

ABOUT THE AUTHOR

Ian Walker

Ian Walker was born in Sydney, Australia but has spent most of his life in the UK. He was, for 26 years, Headmaster of one of the world's oldest schools (founded in 604 AD) and has taught in universities in the UK and USA. He is married to Kerrie, a mathematician turned lawyer; they have a daughter, Hilary, who lives in Sydney and works in cyber-security.

Ian and Kerrie live in a small, rural village in Oxfordshire and spend much of the year in Australia.

BOOKS IN THIS SERIES

William Adams Thrillers

The series tracks the adventures of William Adams, Egyptologist and improbable detective

The Number Of The Beast

Dr William Adams, an Oxford Egyptologist, and Laura Tennett find their lives under threat after the murder of Laura's boyfriend, Jeremy White, a research student whose doctorate Adams is supervising.

While the police seem to be getting nowhere in their investigation, William and Laura escape to a safe house in an attempt to decipher Jeremy's doctoral thesis which may hold a clue to his murder.

They are tracked down by a mysterious organisation operating within the Roman Catholic Church. Their lives are in jeopardy as they discover a secret harboured by the Church for centuries and which threatens to destroy it.

Their travels in England and France lead them to the resting place of one of history's most important caches of religious documents, secured by an ancient sect implacably opposed to the Catholic Church. They discover both the riddle and the solution of Jeremy's death ... and so much more.

The Cylinder Of Babylon

An ancient clay cylinder, covered in cuneiform writing, is discovered by archaeologists in Babylon, in war-torn Iraq. Prof

William Adams is called from Oxford to translate the cylinder and there collaborates with Prof Ellie Green. Further spectacular and widely-publicized finds apparently confirm the history of the Bible.

Terrorist activity forces the dig site to be closed and Adams and Green's lives are threatened.

Adams completes his translation of the cylinder only to find that his discovery could set the combustible world of the Middle East alight. National and international pressure to suppress Adams' findings mount as the cylinder goes missing.

In this dual-voiced narrative, we also learn of the travails of the original seventh-century BC owner of the cylinder and how it comes to be placed in the secret archive rooms under King Nebuchadnezzar's great library.

Loved By The Gods

A sensational discovery in outback Australia leads English academic William Adams, Visiting Professor of Archaeology at the University of Sydney, and his team to investigate.

A chance meeting draws the team into the ambit of the Mangarai, custodians of the country on which the discovery is made.

Tensions develop as the operations of the archaeological team, the Mangarai, Ernest Souter, 'owner' of the land, and would-be developers of the uranium-enriched site, clash.

Two stories of the tribe and team are interwoven as kundela-initiated ritual murders follow abduction and rape. Vengeance, it appears, is never satisfied.

Same Play, Different Actors

Following the death of his wife and daughter, Prof William Adams returns from Australia to Oxford.

Here he receives death threats, and a bungled attempt to kill him leads to the death of three innocent people.

Adams renews his relationship with Dr Robin Atwell and together they escape to Venice to hide from his would-be assassin.

Who can want him dead? What can the motive be?

Will they be able to escape the efforts of an apparently determined murderer?

BOOKS BY THIS AUTHOR

Plato's Euthyphro

A commentary on the Greek text of one of Plato's early dialogues.

Faith And Belief: A Philosophical Appraoch

An assessment of the nature of faith in the Christian tradition.

The Anatomy Of Belief And Unbelief

Agnosticism and atheism, as most commonly understood, represent a misunderstanding of faith and are grounded on self-defeating assumptions. Apart from its application to religious historical tenets, propositional belief has scant place in religion. Yet trying to recover historical propositions in religion is a fruitless exercise.
In religion, there can never be justification. The unbelief which attacks this misguided notion is chasing a chimera. Faith should be seen as a thoroughly natural phenomenon. Metaphysical atheism is as misconceived as metaphysical theism.

The Concept Of Karma - Thinking About Life And Death

Will I survive my death? Does it make any sense to speak of disembodied persons, or souls? Am I free, or are my actions determined? What does karma mean for our understanding of

God, for ethics, for vegetarianism? In The Concept of Karma - Thinking about Life and Death, Ian Walker aims to get behind popular conceptions to the heart of the doctrine as found in Hindu and Buddhist texts and offers answers to all these questions and more.

The M Galaxies Trilogy

Science Fiction
Three books in one: three planets, three murders, cosmic consequences.
Book 1: Lyra - The M57 Galaxy
Science reaches its natural conclusion: the extension of human life to infinite duration. But is the price too high to pay?
On an outworld mining planet, a mysterious scientific institute experiments on bio-replication with fatal consequences.
Book 2: Hyadea - The M45 Galaxy
In a remote, vulnerable village, happenstance determines that all the children become telepaths who come to unite two continents and to dominate life on the planet.
Book 3: Ilium - The M45 Galaxy
The ancestors of the planet are now the greatest power in the Supercluster. They find that their hegemony is threatened by newly discovered, neolithic men.

Printed in Great Britain
by Amazon